The Earl's Comeuppance

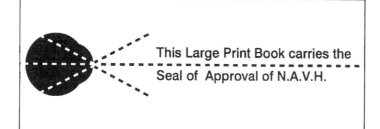

This Large Print Book carries the
Seal of Approval of N.A.V.H.

The Earl's Comeuppance

Phylis Ann Warady

Thorndike Press • Waterville, Maine

All the characters and events portrayed in this work are fictitious.

Published in 2005 by arrangement with Phylis Warady.

Thorndike Press® Large Print Romance.

The tree indicium is a trademark of Thorndike Press.

The text of this Large Print edition is unabridged.
Other aspects of the book may vary from the original edition.

Set in 16 pt. Plantin by Liana M. Walker.

Printed in the United States on permanent paper.

Library of Congress Cataloging-in-Publication Data

Warady, Phylis Ann.
    The earl's comeuppance / by Phylis Ann Warady.
      p. cm.
    ISBN 0-7862-7223-6 (lg. print : hc : alk. paper)
    1. London (England) — Fiction. 2. Mothers and
daughters — Fiction. 3. Nobility — Fiction. 4. Widows —
Fiction. 5. Large type books. I. Title.
PS3573.A65E17 2005
  813'.54—dc22
                                        2004028695

This book is dedicated to my mother,
Henrietta Christina,
and to my longtime patron,
Gordon.

As the Founder/CEO of NAVH, the only national health agency solely devoted to those who, although not totally blind, have an eye disease which could lead to serious visual impairment, I am pleased to recognize Thorndike Press★ as one of the leading publishers in the large print field.

Founded in 1954 in San Francisco to prepare large print textbooks for partially seeing children, NAVH became the pioneer and standard setting agency in the preparation of large type.

Today, those publishers who meet our standards carry the prestigious "Seal of Approval" indicating high quality large print. We are delighted that Thorndike Press is one of the publishers whose titles meet these standards. We are also pleased to recognize the significant contribution Thorndike Press is making in this important and growing field.

Lorraine H. Marchi, L.H.D.
Founder/CEO
NAVH

★ Thorndike Press encompasses the following imprints: Thorndike, Wheeler, Walker and Large Print Press.

1

"Mama, are you certain you wish for us all to leave this snug cottage and go up to London?"

Margaret Astell lifted her gaze from a dove gray morning dress she was refurbishing to deliver a gentle reproof to her firstborn, a needle-witted young miss of eighteen, who sat studying an open ledger resting on a delicately carved escritoire.

"Dearest, pray don't try to wheedle out of our agreement. You gave your word if I invested in the annuities to ensure the boys' education that you'd make your come-out with good grace."

"So I did," Henrietta admitted. "But I keep adding up the columns, and our funds are so limited, I doubt your scheme can succeed."

Margaret pressed a cool hand against her throbbing brow. She was convinced that if she could contrive to introduce Henrietta into London's *ton,* some eligible young nobleman would make her an offer. But to her daughter's mind, such things happened only in fairy tales.

"Henrietta, I consider it poor-spirited of you to continue to tease me." Then, sensing she must tread lightly, Margaret gentled her tone. "If you recall, while I agreed an annuity was necessary for Ned — after all he's at Harrow and will want to go up to Oxford — I differed with you in Toby's case. He's only five. Yet, I haven't nagged you, have I?"

Chagrin crept across Henrietta's fair countenance. "You are entirely in the right. I beg your pardon."

"Which I freely give. Now I trust the matter is closed. Launching you into Society will be difficult enough without you cutting up my peace with futile arguments."

Girlish voices, gaining in volume as they neared the salon, provided a timely diversion. Margaret found herself regarding her twin daughters, gangly thirteen-year-olds. At the threshold, both tugged on a disheveled garment, each determined to dislodge it from her sister's grasp.

"Let go!" Blue eyes flashing, Hannah

gave a defiant toss of flaxen curls. "It's mine I tell you!"

Hester wrinkled her pert, upturned nose. "It was hanging on my side of the closet."

"Rose must have hung it there by mistake. It's mine just the same," Hannah insisted.

"Girls, a little less heat if you please," Margaret admonished. Contemplating the arduous task of converting the two wild hoydens into mannerly young ladies by the time they left the schoolroom — a scant five years hence — made Margaret's spirits sink. A sick headache, looming in the background, now blossomed.

With the callow unconcern of youth, Hannah risked their mother's further disapproval by giving a fresh tug on the disputed dress.

"Hannah! Give me that gown before you tear it."

Hannah, realizing belatedly she'd tried her mother too far, would have gladly obeyed. However, Hester thwarted her twin by keeping her tenacious hold.

"Dare you defy me?" Margaret asked in a quelling tone of voice.

A speaking glance passed between the girls. Together, they advanced and deposited the wrinkled dress in her lap.

"Thank you." Margaret struggled to contain her temper. "Have you girls finished your packing?"

The twins exchanged a guilty look.

"No, ma'am," Hannah responded.

"I don't see why we must share a trunk merely because we are twins," Hester whined.

Patience quite spent, Margaret rounded on them. "Go finish your packing. And if I hear any more raised voices this afternoon, you'll both take bread and milk at the nursery room table for supper!"

As it was now clear as polished crystal that dearest Mama was in a rare taking, the twins retreated in haste. The instant they'd gone, a surge of affection swept through Margaret. Perhaps she'd dealt too harshly with them. Living in each other's pocket, twins were bound to resent each other at times. She plucked the garment from her lap, setting it atop her workbasket.

"Henrietta, do you have any notion which twin this sorry relic belongs to?"

"No, ma'am. Considering its condition, it's no great matter."

"It is ready for the rag bag," Margaret conceded. She finished sewing trim on one cuff of the gray gown and began to pin a row of lace around the other. "They both need new gowns. I'll make some up for them once we are settled in London, where I may take advantage of the marvelous bargains on material bolts at Grafton's."

Henrietta experienced a glow of pride. Her mother's dressmaking skills had long been the talk of the neighborhood. However, recent financial reverses had forced Margaret to temporarily neglect her needle. Indeed, Henrietta reflected, they were lucky to have retained ownership of the manor house and its surrounding acres, presently leased, which would eventually pass to Ned. Watching her mother's comely brown eyes lighten at the mention of London, Henrietta observed, "I collect you've missed the city bustle after living so quiet all these years in the country."

"Indeed, it's much easier to dress stylishly when one lives in the hub of fashion. Though I am sure I don't know what we Astells would have done if my own dear papa had not retired from trade and become a country squire just when John found himself with pockets to let."

While her mother possessed many admirable traits, the quality Henrietta respected most was that she never dwelt upon her deceased husband's shortcomings. The

11

Honorable John Astell, a younger son of the Earl of Skye, had married Margaret, sole off-spring of second-hand-goods dealer, Tobias Hicks, because of her exceptionally generous dowry. Moreover, he had always treated his father-in-law in a condescending manner, even after he'd gambled away Margaret's fortune and had been forced to accept the tradesman's invitation to remove his family from town and reside on his father-in-law's country estate. Thus, while Henrietta had loved her father, she would be the first to admit that he'd lacked character, and had never been more than a charming, irresponsible rogue.

As for her grandfather, although he'd died when Henrietta was thirteen, she remembered him well. Indeed, she attributed her hardheadedness in business matters to Tobias, who'd left the bulk of his fortune invested in cotton. No doubt, he'd reasoned that this plan stood the best chance of ensuring that his daughter and her family would be kept in comfort, in spite of John Astell's spendthrift ways. And, but for the Napoleonic Wars and the recent trouble with the Americans, Grandpapa's plan would have answered. Unfortunately, prolonged hostilities had rendered cotton worthless, due to the loss of the American market and the fact that the Continent was controlled by the French army.

Of course, if Henrietta's father had continued to farm the estate after Tobias's death, they could have eked out a living despite the war. Instead, unable to face debtor's prison, John Astell had put a bullet through his brain, leaving his wife saddled with five offspring.

"It was kind of Grandpapa to invite us to live with him up at the manor house, was it not, Mama?"

"Indeed it was," Margaret agreed.

"I scarcely remember London," said Henrietta.

"I'm not surprised. When we came to live with Papa, you were a mere child, Ned was barely out of leading strings, and the twins were babes in arms."

"I collect Toby wasn't even born yet."

"True. A pity Papa passed away so soon after his namesake's birth."

Henrietta knew that Margaret held the opinion that had her father lived a bit longer, he would have settled a larger portion upon Toby. As things stood, he would inherit only a modest legacy, whereas Ned, as the eldest son, would inherit not only a legacy but also the manor house and immediate grounds as well.

For her part, Henrietta regretted Grandpapa had not provided dowries for his granddaughters in his will. Such a provision would certainly have paved the way for her mother, who was so determined to see all three daughters accepted into Society. However, recounting the past never changed it one jot, so Henrietta decided to turn the conversation.

"What of Rose? Does she go with us to town?"

Rose had moved with them to the cottage, chiefly because their tenants at the manor house didn't care to employ the aged servant.

"No, dearest. She'll bide here at the cottage. The family coach is not well sprung. Her old bones would never stand the journey."

"The family coach? You're joking me, Mama! Travel up to London in that relic?"

"I own it will be an uncomfortable ride, but since the wheelwright's son is making the necessary repairs, we needn't fear a breakdown *en route*. As he wishes to enlist, he has agreed to drive us up to London."

"Wouldn't it be wiser to take the mail coach?"

"I fear it's not quite the thing. In any

case, our purse won't stretch to cover five fares."

Mama was right, thought Henrietta. Taking a public conveyance would set them down in London with too little ready cash. Thank goodness the cost of leasing a town house would be covered by the rental income from the manor. This sum must stretch to cover most of the household expenses as well.

However, once they arrived in town, Henrietta meant to call upon at least two publishers in Fleet Street. In the past, the small sums earned by her pen had helped keep the Astell family afloat. Extra earnings would be especially welcome in London, where everything was reputed to be so much more expensive. She silently resolved to write more articles, at least until Mama became so discouraged by her lack of progress in launching Henrietta into Society, that she consented to their return to the cottage.

As if she could read her daughter's mind, Margaret set aside the dress she'd been trimming and said, somewhat hesitantly, "Before I retire to the kitchen to help Rose with supper, there is another topic I feel must be broached. It's in regard to your scribbling, dearest."

Heart plunging, Henrietta scanned Margaret's face. "Go on, Mama," she said in a low voice.

"Dearest, I freely own the moneys you've earned with your pen have been a godsend, especially after John's death, when I was at wit's end trying to make ends meet."

Margaret shot her daughter a worried look, faintly tinged with remorse as she hurried on. "But, Henrietta, it won't do for you to continue your scribbling while you are making your come-out. You understand, don't you?"

Henrietta fought a sensation of dizziness. The bare bones of a Gothic novel were just beginning to simmer in her mind. How vexing of Mama to forbid her to set pen to paper at this juncture.

Henrietta stifled a sigh. She'd so wanted to try her hand with a heroine similar to those of Mrs. Radcliffe's. Obviously working on a novel was out of the question for the present; however, she might be able to persuade her mother to relent a bit by appealing to her practical nature.

"No one suspects I'm Anne Finch. Where's the harm if I continue to write for the periodicals?"

"Dearest, I appreciate your desire to ease the family finances, but if even a hint, the tiniest rumor, reaches any *ton*nish matron's ears, your reputation will suffer. I cannot allow you to risk ruining your chances. Of course you may write as much as you wish in your journal. Even the highest stickler cannot object to that. However, for the length of the London Season . . . until you are married, I should like your word that you will submit no more articles for publication."

"When I marry? What then?"

Acute pain clouded Margaret's countenance, but it sped past, leaving Henrietta to doubt whether she'd seen that emotion reflected in her mother's face or had merely imagined it.

Margaret, composure regained, replied, "Dearest, perhaps you will be fortunate, and the gentleman you marry will not mind your scribbling once he comes to know you." Henrietta brightened. "Then after a young man fixes an interest upon me, I may ask if he objects?"

"No such thing! Such a discussion is bound to cause mischief. Furthermore, you shall refrain from submitting any more articles for publication until you are safely wed. Is that understood?"

17

"But, Mama, if I don't broach the subject, how am I to know how my betrothed feels?"

Margaret sighed. She had enjoyed her own come-out to the hilt and didn't understand Henrietta's reticence. Come to that, though she dearly loved her eldest, she'd never understood what prompted the child to take up the pen in the first place. Before she could think of a suitable reply, a commotion in the the scullery commanded her attention. Her ears picked up Toby's childish voice, its pitch rising with his mounting excitement.

Bursting into the parlor, Toby exclaimed, "Mama, guess what I've brought home from the pond. Pollywogs!"

Margaret braved a quick glance at the five-year-old boy and let out a low shriek. "Toby! Just look at you. You're soaking wet. What mischief are you embroiled in this time?"

"I told you already," Toby said, in an injured tone. "Pollywogs. Rose said I can't keep them in the scullery, but I can, can't I?" He added in an conspiratorial whisper, "They turn into frogs you know."

Margaret's heart melted. "Yes, I know," she whispered back, then added in her normal tone, "however, they're ever so much more likely to do so outdoors."

His face fell. "I know, Mama, but may I keep them anyway?"

Margaret hid a smile behind her hand. The little rogue was trying to twist her round his finger.

"I can, can't I?" Toby pleaded.

She tried to look stern, but despite all her efforts, her lips twitched. "Yes, you may, but not in the scullery . . . or anyplace else inside the cottage."

"The barn then?"

"How about the pond behind the barn?" Henrietta suggested. "I could help you set up a barricade to keep them happily confined."

Margaret sent her eldest a look of gratitude. "How about it Toby? Will that answer?"

"Yes, ma'am, it will."

Henrietta nudged her brother. "Come, we'd better get started." She smiled at Margaret. "Don't worry about Toby. I'll set his appearance to rights before supper."

"Excellent," Margaret enthused. But as Henrietta reached the archway, sudden recollection of their interrupted discussion prompted her to call out, "Henrietta, just a minute."

Henrietta whirled round to face her

mother. "Yes, Mama."

"In regard to your scribbling, I must have your word, dearest."

"Three more articles are due to appear shortly, Mama. I've already received payment."

Margaret frowned. "That is rather ill timed. We will just have to pray no one gets wind of your *nom de plume*. But after they appear, no more articles or essays. I'll have your word, Henrietta."

"Mama, you have it."

Henrietta turned and stumbled from the room, pushing Toby along before her. "Do hurry, Toby. Mama will fly into a pet if you're not presentable by suppertime."

Margaret stared after her daughter. She hated to see her eldest looking so unhappy. Her mood brightened as she recalled her own come-out. The daring new waltz had been unheard of at the time, but Margaret had had a wonderful Season all the same. Brown eyes sparkling, she rose from her chair. She'd never breathed a word to her children, but the vicar's dashing young wife had taught her the new step. Humming in three-quarter time, for a few blissful minutes Margaret waltzed. She moved with the grace and verve of a young girl as she floated about the shabby salon.

She felt positively giddy once she stopped dancing. Not at all the proper behavior of a matronly widow with five offspring, she told herself sternly. At thirty-seven, she was too old to go kicking up larks. Still, her headache had fled, and she felt more optimistic than she had earlier.

Margaret smiled. Attired in the first stare of fashion with several suitors dancing attendance, Henrietta would soon change her tune. Once she had formed an eligible connection she'd thank her mother for insisting she have a come-out.

2

In the countess's sitting room, Margaret sat with dignified poise on a sofa upholstered in gold satin brocade. "Do cease your endless pacing, dearest."

"Mama, I cannot," Henrietta protested. "If I try to sit, I think I shall jump right out of my skin."

"Very well," Margaret relented. "But mind you're seated when her ladyship enters so you can stand."

Plagued with doubt, Henrietta paced up and down. How she wished they were back at Upper Wimpole rather than inside the Countess of Chilsea's elegant town house overlooking Grosvenor Square.

But what more could she have done? She'd used every argument she could think of in a vain attempt to talk her mother out of calling on their highborn relative — especially as her mother meant to ask the countess to lend her considerable influence to launch Henrietta properly. Why was dearest Mama being so stubborn?

Actually, Henrietta was almost certain she knew the reason. Mama was blue-deviled. Her grand scheme of launching Henrietta into Society was all to pieces. Her long neglect of her school day's friends had come home to roost. In response to her letters, several had written to advise they had no plans to come up to London for the current Season. Those who expected to obviously felt little compunction to take up old ties of friendship — much less help pave the way for Margaret's daughter. Still, Mama had adamantly refused to leave town until she'd applied to her sister-in-law on Henrietta's behalf.

Much as Henrietta deplored her mother's stubbornness, she had to admire her courage. Once inside the fashionable town house, every instinct had warned Henrietta the approaching interview with her high-in-the-instep aunt would prove more ghastly than anything her fertile brain might imagine. Why even the butler was a snob!

Oh well, Mama was in looks this morning. Her buff-colored gown, edged in rich, chocolate piping, flattered her trim figure and set off Margaret's gorgeous complexion and luxuriant chestnut hair. Henrietta glanced down at her new striped poplin walking dress, which she fancied made her hazel eyes appear green. At least they were impeccably attired for their confrontation with her aunt.

As the minute hand on the ormolu clock advanced, Henrietta watched Margaret press thin-soled kid shoes into the deep pile of the Turkey carpet and eye the royal blue window drapings, corded and fringed in gold.

At the sound of advancing footsteps, Henrietta hastily seated herself upon a needlepointed chair. Her eyes flitted to the doorway. There stood her aunt, Henrietta, Lady Chilsea.

From her vantage point, Lady Chilsea grudgingly conceded the ensuing years had dealt kindly with Margaret. She'd managed to keep her schoolgirl figure in spite of five offspring. The countess's icy blue eyes thawed slightly as they lit upon the pretty young miss who was her namesake. She was pleased to see the girl had inherited the Astell family's blond hair and haughty, upturned nose. She could find no fault with their dress, but then she hadn't expected to, since Margaret was reputed to be clever with a needle.

As she advanced further into the room, she pinned a smile on her lips. "Why Margaret, what a surprise! What brings you up from the country?"

"Good day, Lady Chilsea. May I make known to you my eldest daughter, Henrietta."

Her eyes screened by a thick fringe of dark lashes, Henrietta made the countess a proper curtsy. "How do you do, ma'am?"

"Well enough considering the ungodly hour," the countess snapped. Glimpsing her niece's stricken face, she softened her tone, "Pray be seated, child." She shifted her gaze to Margaret. "Do you care for some refreshment?"

"No, thank you. I hope this unannounced call is not too inopportune."

The countess bestowed a bored look upon John's ill-chosen wife. "Since I've a previous engagement, I'd appreciate it you'd dispense with polite chitchat and tell me the purpose of this visit."

Expression grave, Margaret replied, "I'll come right to the point. We're in London so Henrietta may make her come-out. To complicate matters, living quietly in the country, I've lost touch with old ties. As your own pedigree is impeccable, I have come to beg your help in launching Henrietta."

Outraged, her ladyship flushed. To ask a person of her rank to take the daughter of the unfortunate union between John and a cit's daughter under her wing was incredible! At all costs she must squelch this *coming* creature's pretensions with a well-deserved setdown.

"Whyever should I?"

A naked plea in her brown eyes, Margaret said gently, "Because, while my lineage is undeniably humble, she is your niece and namesake."

The countess waxed indignant. "I beg leave to tell you I was not flattered when John chose to name the chit for me. If you think I'll lift one finger to help the granddaughter of a common hawker of second-hand goods, you're sadly mistaken."

Henrietta cried out in an agonized voice, "Mama, I fear we are keeping Lady Chilsea from a previous engagement." An impish impulse caused her to add, "No doubt with some creature who stands in her eyes as a pink of the *ton!*"

The Earl of Pardo, standing in the doorway, spoke. "Thank you, madam, for the compliment."

Henrietta whipped her gaze toward the

threshold. A raven-haired, broad-shouldered nobleman lazed against the door frame, amusement mitigating his sardonic demeanor.

Horrified, the countess blurted, "Lucian! So early. Did not Reeves make you comfortable in the front salon?"

The earl reacted with a crack of laughter as, with laconic grace, he strode deeper into the room. "Reeves left strict orders that I was to await you there, but my deplorable curiosity got the better of me. I followed my ears, so to speak."

Haughty face aflame, a single thought pulsed inside her ladyship's head. How much of the barbed conversation had he overheard?

Henrietta seized the opportunity to suggest pointedly, "Mama, shall we take our leave?"

Margaret gave no sign she heard. She sat on the edge of the sofa as though turned to stone, admiring the cut of the earl's brown superfine coat, which fit his broad shoulders to perfection. Not to mention his buff trousers and polished Hessians.

"Mama!"

A faint smile twitched at the corners of the earl's mouth. "Henny, where are your manners? I'm not acquainted with these ladies."

The countess cast him a suspicious glance. Surely he recalled the tenuous connection between Margaret and herself?

The Earl of Pardo cocked his head expectantly. The glitter of amusement in his dark eyes belied the bland expression on his face.

The wretch! thought the countess. He was enjoying her discomfiture. Just wait. Once they were wed, she'd be sure to even the score. Gathering her scattered wits, she reluctantly made her guests known to each other.

When presented to Margaret, the earl brushed his lips lightly across the back of her hand. A disturbing current coursed through her. Mercifully, once he let go, Margaret's common sense returned. Arising, she agreed with her visibly relieved daughter that it was indeed time to go.

"I'll escort you to your carriage, ma'am," the earl offered.

Catching a jealous glare from the countess, Margaret said, "I beg you will not, sir. Pray remain with Lady Chilsea." She turned to the countess. "Good day, my lady."

Pride shored up Margaret's resolve not to break eye contact first. She might be situated on a lower rung of the social ladder, but she'd done nothing to be ashamed of. She wouldn't have called at all — knowingly risking humiliation — except for her daughter's sake.

"I am sorry I cannot lend my assistance in the matter we discussed," Lady Chilsea said insincerely. "I'm of the opinion it never does to interfere with the established social stratum."

Margaret bit back a reply. "Come, Henrietta," she commanded, before gliding gracefully away.

Henrietta clenched her teeth so hard her jaws ached. Though her haughty aunt deserved a setdown, she refrained, unwilling to put dearest Mama to the blush.

As she approached the exit, Henrietta heard the earl say, "Now I've placed them. The elder is John's widow and the younger his daughter. He married a cit, didn't he? Then gamed away her fortune? Do you mean to keep them hidden from the *ton* or will you sponsor the chit?"

"Have you run mad? A common tradesman's granddaughter? Margaret has her nerve asking me to help fire off her daughter. I won't have my friends

29

laughing behind my back because I foolishly tried to pass off such an unacceptable connection."

"I daresay you are right, Henny," the earl said soothingly. "Shall we turn to other matters?"

Appalled that she had actually halted in her tracks to eavesdrop, Henrietta bolted from the room.

In the hired carriage bound for Wimpole, tears trickled down Margaret's cheeks. "Dear me. What a hash I've made of the affair." She dabbed the corners of her eyes with a lace-edged handkerchief. "You were right, Henrietta. We should never have called. I simply could not resign myself to giving up and returning to the cottage without at least asking your father's people to help. You do understand, don't you, dearest?"

"Of course. Pray don't distress yourself."

"I quite had my heart set on your presentation. It would not have been so difficult if we had not lost our money, for you are so very pretty."

Henrietta made no answer. Margaret let out a shaky sigh. "I daresay there's nothing for it but to pack and go home."

"Yes, Mama."

Henrietta didn't care a fig if she ever attended a fashionable ball, but it had meant so much to her mother. How hateful the countess was! So condescending to Mama, a sweet lady who had never injured anyone in her life.

How it rankled. Inside Henrietta, a molten fury raged.

She could hardly wait to reach Upper Wimpole, so she might slip upstairs to the attic and commit her wrath to paper — her way of releasing overwrought emotion.

As for that conceited earl, how dare he ogle Mama! Especially after looking down his long nose at them with the air of a man eating green fruit. Puffed-up snob. Henrietta found herself wishing someone would give him the comeuppance he so richly deserved.

Meanwhile, inside the stylish mansion on Duke Street, the countess — satisfied that the glass of port the Earl of Pardo had insisted upon, instead of the dish of tea offered, had put him in a receptive frame of mind — awarded her quarry a teasing, feline smile.

"I confess, Lucian, I don't know how to broach the subject. Never have I suffered such mortification."

"May I suggest, Henny, that you cease dropping vague hints and speak plainly?"

"As you wish. I fear our chance meeting at The George has become the latest *on-dit*. I declare I can't attend a rout or an assembly without being subjected to the most cutting stares." She risked a sly peek from veiled blue eyes to assess his reaction.

Devil a bit! An ominous chill crept upward from the earl's curled toes. So his current flirt thought she could maneuver him into the parson's mousetrap, did she? He hadn't managed to escape all manner of womanly wiles for almost forty years to be led meekly to the altar now.

If Henny were a green girl he might feel differently. But this wasn't her first affair, only her current one. His sharp eyes made a quick appraisal of her fading charms. The countess's blond tresses were losing their luster, and tiny lines webbed the corners of her eyes and nicked the skin above her upper lip. Thank God the male of the species aged less rapidly.

Lucian frowned. Hennie's latest start was outside of enough! In his mind, a distant bugle called retreat.

Taking care that no inkling of his decision reflected on his face, he said, "I should not worry over much. It was a chance meeting. The tattlebaskets will be hard put to make more of it than that."

"I assure you, Lucian, you mistake the matter." She dabbed her eyes. "After always taking the utmost care to behave discreetly, it is so horrid to find my reputation in shreds."

"Doing it up too brown, aren't you, my dear?"

"How can you think it? I am ruined, I tell you. Ruined!"

"I collect you have summoned me here this morning to take a hand in this matter."

She brightened perceptibly. "I knew you'd make things right."

"Indeed, I shall," he said stoutly. "Listen closely. It would never do to let the gabblemongers get the upper hand. I plan to behave as though I am completely blameless and strongly suggest you do the same." He raised her hand to his lips. "And just to make sure that the gossips lose interest and pounce on a more promising morsel, I think our wisest course in future is to meet only at public functions. By chance, of course." With that, the Earl of Pardo made the Countess of Chilsea a farewell bow and sauntered out of her elegant town house.

To celebrate his narrow squeak, Lucian decided to take a stroll, motioning his coachman to follow in his barouche. His mind skipped to Margaret Astell. Though she had a daughter old enough for a come-out, she was one female who'd kept her looks. His mind roved over her trim figure. That thick mane of rich brown hair. And those speaking eyes.

The earl reined in his wandering thoughts. Though a cit, she was obviously respectable, and thus, would never accept *carte blanche*. And it wouldn't be seemly for him to form a serious attachment with a female below his station.

His mouth quirked in a rakish grin. Nevertheless, Margaret Astell was a taking thing.

3

Inside the hackney, Henrietta braced her slight body to compensate for the jouncing caused as the hired coach rolled over the cobblestones. Peering out a side window, all the bravado urging her to undertake the questionable errand slowly seeped away, leaving behind an apprehensive young miss lost in thought.

Just before they'd left for town, the publisher of *The Critical Review* had mailed payment for the article she'd written. If only Mr. Lowndes of *The Monthly Magazine* had been as obliging, she need never have embarked on this excursion.

Henrietta frowned. Though accompanied by a footman in deference to the proprieties, what did it signify? A strong, willing lad and son of the hired cook and butler, Luke was a bit empty in his cockloft. Of course, Mama had no objection to the footman bearing Henrietta company on her professed errand, exchanging their books at the lending library, but if she got wind of Henrietta's real errand, she'd be up in the boughs.

The coach jogged down Cockspur and eased onto the Strand. Fresh fears beset her. Suppose she hadn't enough money for the return trip by hired hack? The idea of being set adrift in the steadily worsening neighborhood to make her way home on foot further daunted flagging spirits. And finally, the audacious errand itself sent a shiver up her spine.

The hackney slowed to a stop. The driver scrambled down from his perch. As he handed her from the cab, she surmised that at some point the Strand had become Fleet Street.

"Here we are, miss, all right and tight. Seventy-six Fleet. Six shillings, please."

Dropping the coins into his waiting palm, Henrietta breathed a sigh of relief. She had enough left to pay for a return trip to Mayfair. As the sound of the hack's wheels receded, she fixed her gaze upon the bookshop's display window, bearing its number and gilt-lettered name, Lowndes Printing. She hid a sudden attack of nerves by smoothing the forest green skirt of her high-necked cambric trimmed with black braid.

"This way, Luke. Follow me." With a final tug to straighten a beflowered chip bonnet, Henrietta grasped the brass doorknob and entered the shop.

Diminished light forced her to pause until her eyes adjusted. Gradually she discerned a high counter behind which, deeper into the room, heavy machinery bleated. A murky haze caused by oil lamps pervaded the printshop.

A tall, reed-thin man with a furrowed brow and muttonchop whiskers twisted a path through the maze of presses, wiping ink off his hands on a leather apron. "How may I serve you, miss?" he inquired.

"I wish to speak to Mr. Lowndes."

The furrows dug deeper troughs in his forehead. "May I inquire as to the nature of your business?"

"It's a confidential matter. If you would be so good as to inform him that Miss Finch desires a word with him." Recognition lit the lean, bewhiskered face. "Miss Anne Finch?"

Henrietta nodded.

The man whisked off his apron and made a deep bow. "Delighted to meet you, Miss Finch. I'm Charles Lowndes."

"How do you do, sir?"

Henrietta was disconcerted to note several pressmen and typesetters had halted their work to stare. Though reasonably sure the noise of the machinery prevented their voices from carrying, the workmen's curiosity made her fidget. Thus, she was pleased when Lowndes motioned toward a door set into a side wall and said, "Come, we'll retire to my office where we may talk privately."

Motioning Luke to wait outside, she sailed through the door the printer held open. Lowndes saw her settled in a commodious leather chair before he asked, "Now, my dear Miss Finch, how may I serve you?"

The faint pink in her cheeks darkened, as she fumbled to explain. "Sir, I don't like to be troublesome; however, although my article appeared in your periodical six months ago, I have not yet received payment. The fact is I have recently settled in town and find myself a trifle pressed."

"Upon my soul, I had no notion of it! My bookkeeper suffered a stroke last October, and although I hired another, he hasn't yet managed to unscramble the accounts." He strode to a bell cord and pulled.

A carrot-topped lad, wearing an ink-stained apron, responded.

"Ask Marlow to be so good as to make up a draft in the name of Miss Anne Finch in payment for her article published in the fall issue. Bid him bring it to me here, as the author is on the premises."

The printer's devil's eyes rounded. "If that don't beat all hollow. A female scribbler. Why she ain't much older than me."

"True. I collect you thought only females of ancient vintage could be authors?"

"Yes, or homely ones," the lad agreed.

Noting a delicate flush spreading across Henrietta's face, the printer said, "I fear we are embarrassing the young lady. Go and fetch Marlow."

As the lad closed the door behind him, the printer's steely gaze shifted to Henrietta. His steady regard made her uncomfortable. Fighting an impulse to squirm, she raised her chin and met the printer's searching gaze.

"Pray don't stare, sir."

Lowndes flushed. "Forgive me, Miss Finch. Since you've confided your pressing need of money, I wonder if you should like to try your hand at a work of fiction?"

Henrietta's thoughts turned to the plot for a Gothic romance busily churning in her mind despite all her efforts to call a halt. "You wish me to write a novel?"

"Yes. Romantic works of fiction are amazingly popular with the young ladies. I'd pay handsomely."

Conflicting emotions assailed Henrietta. She'd dreamed of writing a book, though she'd never voiced the idea. After all, in whom could she confide? Certainly not her mother, who took a dim view of her articles. She opened her mouth, intending to decline, and was dumbfounded to hear herself ask, "How much would you pay, sir?"

"One hundred pounds, plus a bonus if the first print run sells out and I bring out a second edition."

One hundred pounds! Enough to keep the entire Astell family for a year. Longer, considering their income from the leased manor. It would be so agreeable not to have to be forever pinching pennies.

Recollection of her promise to her mother shattered the daydream. She'd given her word she wouldn't write while making her come-out. But, despite her promise, a stubborn seed of hope took root. Though Margaret toiled at fever pitch sewing her firstborn a wardrobe of suitable gowns, Henrietta nursed grave doubts that dearest Mama would bring her ambitious plan to fruition. Particularly after the disastrous call they'd paid on the Countess of Chilsea.

"Perhaps you'd feel more at ease, Miss Finch, if I confided I've a sister about your age. Though I'd be pleased if she had your talent and inclination to write, I must admit my dear mother would do her best to discourage her."

Henrietta treated Lowndes to a rueful smile. "Mama is not given to distempered freaks as a rule, but she fears that, should my authorship become known, my chances at the Marriage Mart will sink beyond the pale. Perhaps she is right. In any case, she has asked me to refrain from publishing my pieces for the duration of the Season." She bit her lower lip, then suddenly blurted, "Only it's so difficult, sir, to curb my passion to write."

Hot tears stung behind her eyes. With difficulty, Henrietta managed to contain an impending cloudburst.

"I collect," the printer observed sagely, "your mother has no inkling of how ingrained your need to write is — else she'd never have asked you to stop."

"Very true. She feels keeping a journal gives me sufficient outlet, but I confess nothing equals the satisfaction of seeing one's work in print."

"You *must* try your hand at a novel. Mayhap, I can convince your mother that your book will give her no cause to blush."

Henrietta's hopes soared, but quickly plummeted. She'd given her mother her promise and must abide by it. Unless of course, the family suddenly removed to the country. Only then would she no longer be bound by their agreement.

"May I have some time to consider? I don't wish to make an impulsive decision."

"Certainly, my dear Miss Finch." A knock on the outer door averted his gaze. "Come in."

A stooped, gray-haired man of middle years shuffled in. He took one look at Henrietta and said, "Damme! She must have penned those early pieces in the school-room."

Henrietta blushed.

"Your blunt speech is troubling the young lady. Kindly give her the draft and return to your ledger," the publisher or-dered, curtly.

As the chastised bookkeeper took hasty leave, Henrietta scanned the check. Sat-isfied, she issued a polite smile. "I must be going."

Lowndes offered his arm. "May I escort you to your carriage?"

After a slight hesitation, she was obliged to confess, "I'm afraid I arrived in a hack."

"Never say so."

"Oh dear, that does sound brazen. But think of the comment it would have caused if I'd arrived on your doorstep in the family carriage."

Assuming there was a family carriage to arrive in, Henrietta mused. Truth to tell, the Astell coach had shuddered in its death throes just as they reached London and had been subsequently sold for a paltry sum.

Frowning, the publisher yanked on the bell cord. The carrot-haired printer's devil responded.

"Go out into Fleet and snabble a hack. There's a good lad."

Once the boy took off on his errand, a broad smile eased the grooves etched into Lowndes's forehead as he again offered his arm. This time Henrietta accepted, allowing him to lead her to the front counter of the print shop where Luke sat propped against the wall, dozing, the cloth bag of library books at his feet.

"I must bid you good day here," said Lowndes. "Think over my proposal and let me know your decision."

"I shall," she responded absently, her mind on the library books she'd promised to exchange.

Thirty minutes later, the hack rolled to a halt in front of the lending library. Henrietta gave the correct fare to the coachman and, after bidding Luke to follow her with the books to be returned, hurried inside. She perused the shelves for something suitable for Toby, settling for Swift's *Gulliver's Travels*, which must be read aloud, as Toby's reading ability was not yet equal to it, but dusk was hovering and she had no time to find something he could read on his own.

Dashing from the library, she ran pell-mell into a stately, snow-haired noble-woman, who fixed her sharp blue eyes upon Henrietta. "Gracious, child, you've set my teeth rattling. It's unseemly to rush about knocking your elders off their feet."

"Quite right, ma'am. I apologize for my deplorable manners. You see, I feared I'd be late arriving home. Which is sure to put Mama in a pet. Not that it signifies. There's no excuse for my conduct."

The noblewoman's expression softened. "Fustian! I've sustained no permanent in-jury. Off with you, child. I shouldn't like to be the cause of your mother ringing a peal over you."

"If she does, ma'am, I daresay I deserve it. Are you sure you're all right?"

"Quite sure."

"Then I must fly." With a scant curtsy, Henrietta broke into a walk-run. Luke trailed a few strides behind. Darkness was sure to fall before she reached Upper Wimpole. Mama would wonder what delayed her. She hated to fob her off with a fib, but the truth would overset her already-harried parent more than a white lie.

Lies were strange things, Henrietta mused. There were good lies and bad lies, social lies and malicious lies. But the best lies were long yarns entirely spun from fiction that somehow or other seemed to acquire a mythical kind of truth.

Her footsteps slowed. If only she hadn't promised Mama. The characters in her fevered brain clamored to escape. She felt as if her head were about to explode as in her mind's eye she saw Pamela, her innocent heroine, pitted against the villainous Count di Moro.

"Good evening, Pamela," leered the count.

Pamela racked her brain seeking a graceful way to thwart the wicked intentions of the nefarious villain.

By all that was holy, where was Leonardo when she so desperately needed him?

Henrietta gradually became aware of Luke's hand tugging her sleeve. "Gracious, what is it?" she asked crossly.

"Miss, it be almost dark. Kin we go home?"

She noted the rapidly fading twilight. "Yes, of course. Follow me. Mind you don't drop Toby's book."

Henrietta set off at a brisker pace. Mama would be quite worried. Her chest ached because she daren't pause to catch her breath. Instead, she pressed on, winded, tired, but, unlike Luke, not the least bit intimidated by the enveloping darkness, despite the fact that she had every reason to suspect that the evil genius, Count di Moro, still lurked somewhere in the shadows of her mind just waiting his chance to escape her vigilance.

4

A berlin coach and four, the family crest emblazoned on its side, picked a cautious path over the muddy, pocked road. Viscount Miles Stuart glowered out a side window, unable to see anything except slanting sheets of pelting rain.

Curst bad luck! Miles had broken his journey to look in on his younger brother, Charles. As a result, he'd found himself saddled with the boy's school friend. He'd never have agreed to take on a passenger if he'd thought the weather would turn so treacherous. When they'd set off from Harrow-on-the-Hill a soft April drizzle was falling, but gradually the sky had darkened to an eerie purple and the rain had quickened. The temperature dipped. A bitter wind gave off a haunting wail.

The viscount's piercing blue eyes raked the young stripling seated beside him, dismayed at the boy's chalky pallor and immobile face. He should never have allowed the headmaster to persuade him.

Sensing the viscount's stare, Ned Astell shyly raised brown eyes to meet his benefactor's worried gaze. "Dashed fierce squall, is it not, sir? How much longer before we roll into Kingsbury?" He shivered in spite of a woolen carriage robe tucked about his gangly fourteen-year-old frame.

"It can't be much farther. Buck up, lad." Miles Stuart infused his voice with good cheer for Ned's sake. "Something hot in your stomach will fix you up quicker than you can say 'Jack Robinson.' I daresay a brazier of hot coals to keep your feet warm for the rest of your journey would not go amiss."

"Yes, sir. I don't mean to be a nuisance. Old Palmer's a curst loose screw to have teased you into taking me up to London."

"Don't give it another thought. It's the least I can do to make amends after Charles infected you with his measles. Besides, I'm glad for the company."

The viscount had difficulty quelling a frown. While his brother, Charles, had fully recovered from his bout of measles, Ned was still too pale and painfully thin. The headmaster had confided that the youth,

48

plagued by a racking cough, slept fitfully, thus adroitly persuading Miles he was honor-bound to convey Ned up to London, where he might convalesce under his family's fond care.

Ned embarked on a coughing fit. The viscount's sharp eyes filled with wary concern, and uncertainty roiled in his mind as to whether to drum on the boy's back or not. To his relief, before he could decide, the coughs slackened.

When he could again speak, Ned said, in an injured tone, "I shouldn't be so troublesome if only the weather had held fine."

"Don't tease yourself. Once we reach the inn and chase the chill from your bones before a roaring fire, we'll both recover our spirits. At Kingsbury we shall turn onto Edgeware, an infinitely superior roadway. When we resume our journey, our speed should pick up."

Sensing the carriage slowing, the viscount peered out a side window. "Ah, it appears we have arrived."

Forty-five minutes later, Miles eased back in a Windsor chair, situated in a private parlor off the main tavern. "Have a little more of the oxtail soup," he urged.

"No thanks."

"A wedge of the Stilton?"

49

Ned shook his head. "Since I fell ill, my appetite has not been wonderful. I prefer to nurse the hot toddy you ordered to warm me up. It soothes my scratchy throat."

Miles eyed the youth seated across the plank table. In spite of a sickly pallor, the Astell lad was handsome, having thick, chestnut brown hair, mischievous brown eyes, and a finely chiseled nose. "You do look a trifle pulled. Though I've no doubt your family will soon have you fit."

"Quite right, sir. Between Mama and my sisters I shall soon be in plump currant."

"How many sisters do you have?" the viscount inquired laconically. He encouraged Ned to provide details of his family background, not because of an avid interest, but merely to pass the time while a fresh team could be harnessed to his coach.

"Three, my lord. Henrietta's eighteen and my favorite. The twins are a year younger than me, two pretty caper-wits, upon my honor. I've a brother, too. Toby's five."

"And your mother and father, of course."

"Papa . . . died last spring. I think Mama's decided to come out of mourning. It wouldn't answer in town as she wishes to launch Henrietta into Society and will need to chaperone her everywhere."

"I see."

"I don't think you do, sir. Papa . . . Papa . . ." Dark, curly lashes rushed to veil tears welling in Ned's eyes.

Not wishing to embarrass the boy further, Miles refrained from offering his condolences, electing to turn the conversation instead. "You said Henrietta's your favorite sister, I believe?"

"Yes. She's a scribbler, you know," Ned confided in an awed tone, pride creeping into his voice as he added, "Her pieces have been published in many periodicals."

"Amazing!" The viscount's interest perked up. "A bluestocking I collect?"

"A what, sir?"

"A female intellectual."

"Henrietta?" Ned looked perplexed. "I think not. I tried to teach her a little Latin and Greek, but it didn't seem to take. She just seems to have a knack for scribbling is all. I daresay she can't help it, something Mama will not understand. In my sister's last letter, she says she's forbidden to write anyplace but in her journal while she is making a come-out."

"I daresay your mother doesn't want to ruin her chance of interesting some eligible gentleman in marrying her. Your sister's scribbling is a trifle *extraordinaire*."

"Well she may not be the usual milk-and-water female, but at least she's not a crashing bore. I think it a bit hard that Mama curbs her scribbling."

"Has your sister agreed to follow your mother's wishes in this matter?"

"Yes, even though she feels that nothing will come of Mama's scheme and that no gentleman will offer because of her lack of a dowry."

The clump of approaching boots diverted the viscount's attention. "Ah, Buxton, are the horses ready?"

"Yes, my lord. Being as you want to set the lad down in Wimpole Street, I intend to take Marylebone Road when it crosses Edgeware."

"Very wise, Buxton. We shall join you at the coach directly."

Soon after they'd resettled inside the berlin, Ned drifted off to sleep, not waking even when Buxton halted the carriage before the designated number on Upper Wimpole at around four that afternoon. The viscount studied the Georgian structure with a sophisticated eye, taking in the genteel overall shabbiness of a neighborhood inhabited by respectable tradesmen.

Dispatching Buxton to the front door to make certain they'd reached the right abode, Miles gently shook his youthful companion's thin shoulder.

"What?" Ned opened bewildered, disoriented eyes.

"Steady lad. I believe we've arrived at the house your family has hired for the Season."

Once Buxton verified the address, he hurried back to open the carriage door. Ned's descent was rather clumsy as he was not yet wholly awake. The viscount insisted the frail lad lean on him for support as they advanced through the entrance door, held wide open by Jonas, the portly, florid-faced butler, whose neat gray livery betrayed a stomach paunch.

All solicitude once he understood he was speaking to young Master Ned, Jonas saw them comfortably ensconced in the front sitting room, before he excused himself to ferret out Miss Henrietta, who — unless he missed his guess — was up in the attic scribbling away. However, as she was the only Astell presently at home, he had no choice but to tackle the successive flights of stairs.

Inside the attic, Henrietta sat at a rickety old desk, lost in the intricacies of her tangled plot.

"Visitors, Miss Astell," Jonas announced, permitting himself a martyr's sigh, once he'd stopped wheezing.

Henrietta was not best pleased by the interruption. "I warn you, Jonas, this had better be important." Her scowl gave way to a pensive expression. "Did you say visitors?"

Jonas nodded.

"Impossible. We don't know anyone in London."

"It's Master Ned, miss."

"Gracious! Why didn't you say so at once?"

Belowstairs, the viscount's acute ears picked up the sound of light, swiftly approaching feet just before a blond, sweet-faced young miss burst into the sitting room.

"Ned!" she cried, rushing to envelop her brother in a hug. Drawing back, she appeared bewildered. "Whatever brings you to town?" A sharp assessing look failed to allay her agitation. "Gracious, you're nothing but skin and bones! Have you been ill?"

"Henrietta, give over. I've had the measles. Old Palmer insisted I come home so you can fatten me up."

"And so we shall."

Miles suffered through Ned's halting introduction. He considered his patience justly rewarded when Henrietta acknowledged him with a winsome smile.

"How is it, sir, that you came to be burdened with the troublesome job of bringing Ned up to town?"

Miles was bemused by the gleam of intelligence in her striking hazel eyes. In truth, he'd expected, undoubtedly due to a prejudice against female authors, a plain-faced young lady dressed like a dowd. His keen blue eyes scrutinized her slim, comely figure, approving her snuff-brown afternoon dress enhanced by blond lace trim. Miss Astell possessed a pertly upturned nose, upon which Miles was beguiled to note a smudge of ink. Her right hand, too, bore a few, telltale smudges, causing him to deduce that she'd been writing when unexpectedly interrupted.

"Ned's been no trouble. Indeed, I found his conversation quite interesting." A glitter of amusement warmed his eyes.

"You are very kind." Her smile faded as she shifted her gaze to Ned. "As usual, your tongue runs on wheels. I daresay you bored the viscount to tears with your prattle."

Flushing, Ned tugged at his neckcloth as if it were suddenly too tight. Miles found himself inordinately pleased when, having noted her brother's discomfiture, Henrietta swiftly relented.

"Never mind. You're forgiven. I imagine you will want something to eat after your journey."

"Famous! I vow my appetite's back."

Henrietta shifted her gaze to Miles. "Lord Stuart, will you not join us?"

"If it will not put your cook all on end, yes."

"Mrs. Jonas? Nothing ruffles her feathers. I declare she's the best bit of luck we've had since we began our ill-starred venture up to town."

"Will you excuse me a moment? I must have a word with my coachman first."

"Certainly, my lord," she said, pulling the bell cord.

Soon after Miles exited, the butler responded to her summons.

"Jonas, will you ask Mrs. Jonas to prepare a light repast for three?"

"Very good, miss."

Once he'd left them, Ned observed, "I take it Mama's plan to launch you before the *ton* has gone awry."

Henrietta sobered. "True. She's at a standstill."

"What happened?"

"When Mama realized she was making no headway on her own, she insisted upon calling on Lady Chilsea. I accompanied her. It was ghastly."

"I imagine the countess acted very top-lofty?"

"Aunt Henrietta was needlessly cruel, but at least she made Mama realize there is simply no way her plan can carry. We've begun to pack against our removal to the country."

Henrietta's eyes filled with concern. "Your coming will delay our departure, I collect, for you are not up to the journey." Her countenance brightened. "No matter. The rent has been paid for the season so there's no hurry."

"Bad as that is it?" Ned asked glumly.

"Bad as what?" Miles inquired from the threshold, then flushed with embarrassment as he belatedly realized the impropriety of his question. "I beg your pardon. I daresay it is none of my business."

A rosy blush stained Henrietta's cheeks. "Not at all, sir. I was merely bringing Ned up to date on the family doings," she responded lightly. Then, noting the viscount was still standing, exclaimed, "Gracious, how rag-mannered of me. Pray be seated."

"After you, Miss Astell." Miles motioned

her to seat herself first. Only when she'd complied did he oblige by following suit and, with a nonchalant air of a young man skilled at putting others at ease, set out to charm her. "Ned tells me you're in London to make your bow to Society. I would imagine someone as pretty as you has the entire *ton* at her feet."

Henrietta's cheeks turned a deeper shade of pink. "I beg you not to spout such nonsense. There is no reason why Society should express the least interest in me. Not to wrap the affair in cotton, I've no dowry, and, to make me even less eligible, my grandfather was in trade."

Miles grinned, admiring her candor. "Surely there is *something* in your character to recommend you, Miss Astell?"

She shook her head. "Nothing I can think of, sir."

"Where is everybody, anyway?" Ned asked.

Henrietta brightened. "On a tour of Westminster Abbey. Mama's been toiling away ever since we arrived. She's sewn each of us a wardrobe of stylish clothes she anticipated we should need, and, consequently, there's been no time for outings. So I'm delighted that they went off today on a purely pleasurable excursion."

"You did not accompany them, Miss Astell?" asked Miles.

A guilty look cropped up on her pretty face. "No, sir. I'm recovering from a slight cold."

The viscount astutely avoided mentioning the smudge on her pert nose that hinted a different reason why she'd elected to stay home. He'd been on the verge of teasing her about it, when he realized it might embarrass her. Ned had not sworn him to secrecy about his sister's scribbling; however, the viscount had to own that the lad had been a bit indiscreet in confiding personal information to a comparative stranger.

After an excellent tea, Miles arose with lanky grace. "Miss Astell, may I call in a day or so to see how this stripling does and to pay my respects to your mother?"

Henrietta rewarded his request with a sunny smile. "Indeed, sir, I am sure that would please Mama. She will want to thank you herself for being so kind to Ned."

Miles's sharp gaze drank in every particular of the intriguing young miss — the better to tide him over the next few days until he might properly call again.

In the carriage, heading toward Mayfair, the viscount could not help grinning.

Imagine. The lovely Miss Astell was actually a female scribbler. How diverting.

But seconds later, he was no longer grinning. If his sharp ears hadn't deceived him, the Countess of Chilsea's refusal to sponsor her niece smacked of spite pure and simple. The viscount's eyes narrowed. Unless, of course, the pert young miss's mother was just too awful to tolerate socially. However, since both Henrietta and Ned were well mannered, he doubted their mother could be *too* vulgar. In any case, since he meant to call again in Wimpole Street as soon as he dared, he'd then be in a position to judge Mrs. Astell's social graces for himself.

Provided Henrietta's mother was as unexceptional as he hoped, it might be amusing to open a few of Society's doors presently closed to the Astells. Certainly the family had sailed rough seas of late. It would scarcely inconvenience him to put himself out a bit for their sake. Besides, it would give him a good excuse to see more of the young minx who had, at least temporarily, captured his attention.

5

"Be candid, dearest. Do you think the occasion merits wearing the emeralds or not?"

Henrietta left off the delicate task of drawing on expensive silk stockings to study Margaret's appearance. The rich green satin gown seemed admirably suited to Margaret's mature figure. Her dainty feet were clad in thin silver slippers, and she carried a fan which had strips of silver worked into its design.

An emerald necklace, comprised of small, matched stones set in delicate filigrees of silver, encircled her creamy neck. Apparently, she harbored some doubt as to the propriety of wearing her sole piece of really good jewelry, even though it complemented her gown.

"Considering that we are attending a performance of the Italian opera at Covent Garden, I believe your emeralds are appropriate. Do wear them by all means."

"I am so glad you agree. Now allow me to lend you a hand with your toilette."

With infinite care, Margaret eased a pale gold, cobweb silk over her daughter's head, adjusting the gathered bodice and fluffing the short sleeves. She eyed the straight skirt with modified train to be sure it fell properly, and finally satisfied, suggested, "Sit down, dearest, so I may arrange your hair. Shall I coil it at the crown and perhaps allow a few curls at the temples?"

"As you wish."

Pulling a brush through Henrietta's hair, Margaret observed, "Who would dream that Ned's measles would account for such a fortuitous upturn? Due to Lord Stuart's kindness, we have been showered with invitations."

"Be that as it may, Mama, what does it signify? I still have no dowry, and without one my chance of receiving an offer is unlikely."

The brush in Margaret's hand hesitated, and then continued through her daughter's golden tresses. "Dearest, do you not think that perhaps the viscount is interested in you himself? I daresay he's rich enough to overlook your lack of a dowry, provided he cares for you."

"I shouldn't refine upon it if I were you, Mama. Most of the outings he's arranged have included all the Astells. I've not been singled out for any marked attention."

"Oh, but, dearest, it would be most improper for him to do so, so early. Besides, the entire family was not invited to several evening parties and that *alfresco* breakfast. Only you were, my love, and I as your chaperone, of course. On each of those occasions, Lord Stuart called and personally escorted us. To me, that is very marked attention."

Henrietta nobly refrained from attacking her mother's shaky logic, offering instead, "Lord Stuart realizes we cannot afford a carriage and is merely being thoughtful. I shall ever be grateful to him for paving my way, I assure you." She cast a fond glance at her mother. "I should have hated to retire to our cottage without a chance to show off the exquisite gowns you've contrived with such meager means. I freely admit, though I never dreamed I should, I've enjoyed cutting a modest dash in Society."

Margaret glowed at the compliment, choosing not to contradict her daughter as to whether the viscount's attentions were of a serious nature or not, though her demeanor suggested she thought Henrietta was being overly demure. "Shall I fix the tortoiseshell comb in your hair, or shall you wear your pearls?"

"The pearls, I believe."

As soon as Margaret had secured the clasp of a single strand of tiny pearls, Henrietta rose and began to collect her reticule, ivory fan, and cashmere shawl. "Shall we go down? The viscount's carriage shall soon draw up to our door."

"By all means. I'm quite looking forward to this evening's performance."

As the berlin coach bowled smoothly along, Henrietta was tempted to pinch herself to be sure she was not air-dreaming. In a fortnight, she'd attended a dinner party, an assembly, a rout, and two *alfresco* breakfasts. In addition, the entire family had been borne to the Tower of London to admire, as best they might, a motley menagerie of wild animals and several dank cells, where various members of the nobility had murmured their last prayers. However, all these outings dimmed when compared to the occasions when Lord Stuart had called for her in his pale yellow phaeton, drawn by a pair of roan-colored horses.

A sharp jab of excitement pierced her heart as she recalled their promenade along Rotten Row during the fashionable hour. Lord Stuart had not yet invited her to take the ribbons, but she had not quite lost hope that he might offer to teach her on some future drive.

The carriage stopped. The coachman let down the steps. The viscount descended, then assisted both ladies to alight.

Their party barely reached their box before the lights dimmed and the curtain rose. The clear soprano voice that floated from the stage enchanted Henrietta. A pleasant surprise. Having no musical talents herself, she had not thought she would receive such enjoyment from merely listening. Indeed, she was so awed by the famed Italian signora's voice that it vexed her unreasonably when the curtain descended for intermission.

Miles climbed to his feet and smiled affably. "Shall we promenade, ladies?"

They strolled three abreast across the lobby toward the billowing throng converged about the refreshment stall. The viscount found an alcove and suggested the ladies wait there out of the crush while he fetched their lemonade.

Henrietta watched Miles saunter forth,

his height, broad shoulders, and black hair discernible until he merged with the milling figures. Next, she studied passing faces at random, trying to read some hint of their character in their expressions. She gave a rueful sigh. When her family had packed their trunks against their removal to the country, she'd begun work on her novel. Unfortunately, when it had become clear that Lord Stuart would pave her way into the *ton,* Henrietta hadn't been able to set the book aside in spite of her promise.

However, for several days now she'd been at a standstill, and thought perhaps close scrutiny of the fashionable creatures milling about might help break the impasse. Having always lived in the country until a few months past, she'd become rusticated. What she needed to write a convincing work of fiction was to absorb all she could of the mannerisms and attitudes of contemporary Society. Else how was she to write a novel that would suit a typical young miss's taste?

"Are you taking in the marvelous gowns, as I am, Henrietta?" Margaret asked.

Guilt pangs rippled through Henrietta. Put to the blush, she fanned burning cheeks, thankfully noting Margaret's gaze remained focused at a distance.

"Yes, aren't they lovely."

"Gracious! I believe I see the Earl of Pardo. You remember him, don't you dearest? We met him at your aunt's."

"Of a certainty. How could I ever forget that high-in-the-instep nobleman? Where is he?"

"I've lost sight of him. Shall I tell you if I see him again?"

"No, I believe Lord Stuart is returning. No sign of our punch, but he has a lady with him."

As the viscount neared, Henrietta recognized her. The selfsame lady she'd almost knocked to the ground in her unpardonable rush from the lending library several weeks ago. How abysmally mortifying!

Miles smiled fondly at the snowy-haired gentlewoman on his arm. "Mama, allow me to make known to you the Honorable Mrs. Astell and her daughter, Miss Henrietta Astell. Mrs. Astell, may I present my mother, Lady Stuart."

Insides churning, Henrietta sketched a curtsy. Whatever would the viscount think of her rag-manners when he learned she'd nearly knocked his mother down? And poor Mama. When told, she'd sink with embarrassment.

"How do you do, Mrs. Astell?" Lady

Stuart offered her hand. "Miles has spoken of you and your lovely daughter." Her glance briefly touched Henrietta. "And of Ned as well. I am sorry my Charles gave him the measles, but I understand your son is nearly recovered."

"Indeed, he'll soon be strong enough to return to Harrow," Margaret responded.

Her ladyship fixed her gaze upon Henrietta. "I believe our paths crossed at Hookham's?"

The twinkle in her frost blue eyes grew more pronounced as she smiled encouragingly at Henrietta, who remained in a quake until it dawned on her that Lady Stuart did not mean to give her away.

"We met quite informally on that occasion," Lady Stuart observed, "and though we were not introduced, I was much struck." Her ladyship could not quite stifle a giggle. She carried on with a defiant expression in her eyes that dared anyone to call her to account. "Much struck by your daughter's exuberance. So refreshing. Perhaps you will both call on me one afternoon?"

"Oh, yes. That is, I should love to, my lady." Henrietta slanted a sidelong glance at her mother, seeking approval. Margaret nodded.

"It is settled then. Miles will fetch you,"

said her ladyship. The clearing of a masculine throat behind her caused her to wheel about. "Ah, there you are, Lucian, with our punch at long last. I was beginning to think the curtain would rise before it came."

Sighting the Earl of Pardo balancing a small round tray that held five crystal-cut cups of lemonade, Margaret made a faint gasp.

"Lucian, allow me to make these ladies known to you."

"No need, coz," the earl replied as he handed round the cups. "We met on a previous occasion." The corners of his mouth twisted, giving his face a faintly sardonic mien.

A prickly sensation crept up Henrietta's spine as she noted that the earl's gaze was riveted upon Margaret, causing a delicate pink hue to highlight her mother's creamy skin.

As for Margaret, a delicious shiver raced through her willowy frame, and to her further bewilderment, her eyes seemed to be locked in his mesmeric stare. But what was truly upsetting was the daunting realization that she didn't entertain the smallest wish to break the spell.

"Lucian. I had no idea you would be attending the opera tonight."

Margaret started. Good heavens! Her sister-in-law, the Countess of Chilsea. Margaret could scarcely believe her ill luck.

The earl sketched a careless bow, and with a cynical gleam in his dark eyes, said, "Good evening, Hennie. No need to introduce you, I collect. Naturally you are acquainted with your own sister-in-law and niece."

Lady Chilsea favored him with an icy stare that Margaret was amused to see failed to ruffle his composure one whit. He turned to Lady Stuart. "Aunt Min, I believe the second act is about to start. May I escort you back to your box?"

"An excellent notion, Lucian. I was delighted to make your acquaintance, Mrs. Astell. I look forward to receiving you and Miss Astell."

Henrietta barely noticed Lady Stuart's departure. Her main attention remained fixed upon her aunt, who stood statue still, her envious blue eyes glued upon Margaret's emeralds. The countess covets Mama's necklace! Acute trepidation rippled through Henrietta.

"Coming, Miss Astell?" Miles inquired gently as a distant bell warned that the curtain was about to rise.

The sound must have filtered into Lady Chilsea's avaricious mind, for she suddenly seemed to recollect that she was standing in a public lobby, and thus subjected to many curious stares. Henrietta could only suppose her aunt had reconsidered whatever rash step she'd contemplated, for with a final withering glare, the countess withdrew.

Only then, did Henrietta yield to the gentle pressure on her arm and allow the viscount to lead her back to their reserved box.

There, taking advantage of the theater's hubbub as the audience resettled, she leaned forward and whispered in Margaret's ear. "Mama, why did the countess stare so oddly at your emeralds?"

"Your aunt covets them." Margaret squared her shoulders. "Well, she shan't have my emeralds. They're the only thing of value I ever received from your father's people. I shall never part with them."

"Indeed not. Whyever should you, Mama?" Henrietta responded feelingly.

"Hush, dearest, the curtain is rising."

Henrietta lapsed into silence, preoccupied with a fresh worry. The Earl of Pardo had referred to the viscount as "coz" and to his mother as "Aunt Min." Agitated, she fanned her ashen face. Though she'd tried to dismiss her mother's hint that the viscount might have fixed his interest upon her, secretly Henrietta hoped he had.

And now this. He and the earl were cousins. Even if there had been no verbal hints as to the connection, she was now forcibly struck by the family resemblance and could only wonder why she hadn't seen it before.

Of course, to her mind Miles Stuart was infinitely superior. Though their builds were similar, the viscount possessed ingenuous blue eyes and a breezy open manner. Not so the earl, whose cool black gaze and rapier tongue betrayed a cynical turn of mind. Botheration! They would have to be related.

Troubled, Henrietta nibbled on her lower lip, certain the snobbish earl could not like his cousin courting her, a mere nobody. She could only hope that Lord Stuart put no great store in his cousin's opinions.

6

A week later, Margaret presided over the tea table in the sitting room of the house she had rented for the London Season. Beside her squirmed her youngest, Toby, who paid scant attention to the female chitchat rebounding across the table, being preoccupied with eating as many of the thin, crisp biscuits — situated tantalizingly close to his upturned nose — as he could manage without incurring a censorious rebuke from his mother.

Opposite Margaret, a Miss Potts sat primly erect, lace cap proclaiming her spinsterhood perched upon her graying head. Enid Potts, a girlhood friend, dating from when they had attended the same ladies' seminary, proceeded to astonish her hostess with her ravenous appetite. Margaret scarcely knew where to look as the spinster consumed three cream buns and four cups of India tea.

Though amazed, Margaret schooled her countenance to keep its bland facade, while she surveyed her old friend's drawn face through lowered lashes. Is it possible Enid's actually starving, she mused. Yet the brown woolen walking dress and modest accessories bespoke quality. Perplexed, Margaret wondered how to make discreet probes — wishing to help if Enid were in dire straits — but not wishing to pry.

Meanwhile, Enid, her appetite apparently sated, began a leisurely inspection of the room. Gradually, the gaunt face grew animated, and her tightly pressed lips relaxed.

"My dear, I vow I never expected to see such a stylish room in this part of town."

Margaret bristled. "As to my neighbors, though I own they're chiefly tradesmen, I am persuaded they are respectable."

"Dear me, I didn't mean to hint otherwise. Only to compliment you on a sitting room such as I'd expect to find in more *ton*nish surroundings."

Slightly mollified, Margaret responded, "I concede the location's not quite the thing. However, the rents the agent quoted to reside in Mayfair proved too steep."

"Oh?" Disbelief dominated the spinster's thin face. "Did you not inherit your father's fortune when he died?"

Dejection filled Margaret's soft, brown eyes. "Papa left his money in trust with the principle invested in cotton. Last year due to the lack of a ready market, we lost it all."

"How very distressing." Sudden tears popped into the spinster's tiny, black eyes. In a flurry, she dug into her reticule seeking her handkerchief.

Touched by her friend's reaction, Margaret reached across the tea table to clasp her hand. "I appreciate your concern, but the Astells aren't the only family to suffer heavy losses due to the war on the Continent."

"Dearest Margaret, you think too well of me." Enid emitted a sound halfway between a sob and a chuckle. "I confess when I received your note inviting me to tea, I thought my luck had taken an upturn. Instead you've dashed my last hope. To speak plainly, I, too, have suffered grave reverses and hoped you might lend me enough to tide me over until I obtain a post."

No wonder Enid had gobbled up nearly everything off the tea table. She *was* hungry. "Are you in arrears with your obligations?" Margaret queried gently.

"Gracious no! The picture's not that

black. As you know, when I left school I had to make my own way. Lady Barbara was so kind I truly never minded being her companion. However, when she succumbed along with her husband after a carriage accident, I decided to make a fresh start." Enid dabbed at her eyes. "I used my savings to set up an establishment on Baker just off Oxford. Unfortunately, though I'm clever with a needle, I found I've no talent for design. Thus, my venture was doomed to fail."

"My dear, Enid, what a pity my own needs are so pressing. If only my purse were plumper."

An expression of chagrin dominated the spinster's gaunt face. "How thoughtless of me to bore you with my gloomy affairs. Toby looks to be a sturdy lad, but what of your other offspring? And, before it slips my mind, where did you get the Hepplewhite chairs?"

A becoming blush stained Margaret's flawless skin. "I ran across them in a second-hand shop where I managed to acquire them dagger cheap. Papa used to say I'd inherited his eye for fine wood and a graceful line, though I am sure my taste will never equal his."

Enid attempted a smile. "Nonsense. You're every bit as good if this room's a sample. The chair seats look newly uphol-stered. Did you recover them?"

"Yes. I also fashioned the window cover-ings. Ned and Toby helped me hang fresh wallpaper."

"Famous! Though it's a lot of expense to sink into a rented establishment."

"I managed to keep the cost down by doing most of the work myself. I require a room where I may receive callers without being mortified. You see, my eldest daughter is making her come-out."

"I had no inkling Henrietta had left the schoolroom. A pretty child, as I recall."

"Who's grown into a comely young miss whom I pray will make a suitable match. Such an event would go a long way toward repairing the family coffers."

"She has a dowry?"

The smile vanished from Margaret's face. "Would that it were true. My task would be so much simpler."

"But my dear, how do you expect to launch her without one?"

Margaret brightened perceptibly. "Do you know Enid, I'd nearly given up my scheme to present Henrietta when the most famous piece of luck dropped into my lap. You see, Ned took sick with the measles." She pro-ceeded to fill her old friend in with all the details of their chance meeting with Viscount Stuart and his many kindnesses, particularly the trouble he'd taken to ensure that Henrietta receive the *right* invitations. "It is too bad that you have missed the viscount. Today he's transporting Ned back to Harrow."

"How kind of him, to be sure. It is possible he's developed a *tendre* for Henrietta?"

Margaret lowered her eyes demurely. "I daresay I'd be in the alts if he declared himself. But it's early days yet. Nothing is settled. I confess I will be so relieved if Henrietta fixes her interest on any worthy young eligible, for I cannot imagine how I shall manage to launch the twins in a few years unless she succeeds."

She eyed the spinster thoughtfully. "Enid, I've hit on a scheme that may work to our mutual advantage. While I've no funds to spare, there is plenty of room under this roof. What if I offered room and board in exchange for your help with the mountain of sewing I've undertaken to keep Henrietta outfitted?"

Enid's homely face lit up at the suggestion. "I should like it above all things! I don't have money put by to pay next month's lodgings. If I move in with you, that worry will be lifted off my shoulders. Besides, I am sure I could be useful. Not just with the sewing either. I can bear Henrietta company when you are indisposed."

"You understand I shall need you for the remainder of the Season? Is that agreeable?"

"Yes. It allows me sufficient time to obtain a new post without being taxed by money worries."

"It is settled then." With a warm smile, Margaret reached across the table to pat the spinster's hand. From the corner of her eye, a furtive movement diverted her.

"Toby! Haven't you had enough to eat without trying to filch the last cream bun? Whatever will Miss Potts think of your manners?"

"No need to fly up into the boughs, Mama. She ate three."

Ready to sink, Margaret said sternly, "Young man, you will apologize to Miss Potts. Once you have, you will withdraw from our presence. Is that clear?"

"Yes, Mama," Toby said in a hushed voice. He mumbled an apology and took hasty leave.

Margaret winged a concerned glance across the table, gratified to see some of the fiery color had faded from her friend's cheeks. "Enid, I am so sorry."

"Not at all. I shall be happy to excuse Toby's candor if you will forgive me for gobbling up all the sweets. In truth, *my* manners were not overly nice."

"Fiddle. You were truly hungry. I daresay Toby didn't mean to be cruel."

"He's very young. Pray don't refine too much on his small lapse."

The murmur of girlish chatter wafted into the room. "I believe my daughters have returned from their outing."

The Astell twins entered in an unseemly rush; Henrietta trailed them at a more ladylike pace.

"Oh, you've had tea." Hester's face reflected disappointment. "I declare I'm famished. May I have the cream bun, Mama?"

"You may share it with Hannah in the kitchen. But first, I wish to make you known to my dear friend, Miss Potts."

All three sisters curtsied.

"Such pretty daughters, my dear." Enid enthused. "Though I do think it a trifle unfair that none of your offspring inherited either your coloring or your classical features."

"With the exception of Ned, ma'am," Henrietta ventured to say. "He has

Mama's chestnut hair and straight nose." Margaret's gaze lingered upon the twins. How mortifying! Instead of one of their new gowns, they wore faded, ill-fitting dresses. "Girls, please clear away the tea table for cook, who has so much to attend to."

"But Mama, we've not had any tea," Hester protested.

Margaret laughed. "When you've cleared the remains of ours, you may retire to the kitchen where Mrs. Jonas has set aside a platter of treats against your return." Her glance swept to her eldest. "Henrietta, you may join Enid and me, if you prefer."

Henrietta smiled. "I think I'd best preside over the other tea table. As you mentioned, Mrs. Jonas has enough to occupy her without being teased into an hysterical fit." She directed a nod toward Miss Potts. "A pleasure to meet you, ma'am."

The twins, anxious to finish their assigned task so they might enjoy their anticipated treat, scooped up as many dishes as they could safely carry. Bearing the empty teapot, Henrietta managed a more dignified exit.

Enid beamed. "Your eldest is a well-mannered young lady. I congratulate you."

"Now do you see why I think she will make a success of her come-out?"

"Indeed, I shall do everything I can to help." Rising, the spinster began to draw on her gloves. "Margaret, I've enjoyed this immensely."

"You're not going so soon?"

"If you are serious about me moving in, I must pack. When do you wish me to come?"

"As soon as possible. What with the Season coming into full swing, there is so much to do."

"Together, we'll manage nicely, I am persuaded. Would Wednesday next be a convenient time for me to move in?"

"Wednesday's fine," Margaret agreed, a bit worried as to how Enid would fare for the four intervening days. "If you send round a note, I can dispatch Jonas to Baker Street to lend a hand with your trunk."

"No such thing. I shall arrive in a hack. Only then does Jonas have my leave to wrestle with my baggage."

"As you wish," Margaret capitulated.

After Enid left, Margaret lingered in the sitting room, gratified that the spinster would be helping with the endless sewing. Besides, she needn't be vexed to death wondering how her friend was faring.

Hearing a faint wheeze, Margaret looked up. "Yes, Jonas, what is it?"

"A gentleman in the anteroom desires a private word, ma'am. Shall I show him in?"

"A gentleman? Are you sure he is not calling upon Henrietta?"

"No, ma'am. It's Mrs. Astell the Earl of Pardo wishes to speak with."

Margaret blinked. If Jonas had announced the Prince Regent himself had come calling, she couldn't have been more startled. She sighed. She supposed there was no putting him off. "Very well, Jonas, show him in."

The earl hesitated at the threshold. Moving forward to greet him, Margaret was pleased to detect a glimmer of admiration in his dark eyes as he perused the room's furnishings. When his arresting gaze came to focus solely upon her, Margaret did her best to ignore her erratic heartbeats. Outwardly calm, she willed herself to perform the duties of a proper hostess with aplomb.

"Do be seated, my lord."

The earl shrugged his lanky frame into the nearest Hepplewhite.

"Would you care for some refreshment?"

"No thank you, ma'am."

"Are you certain? I assure you it's no trouble to ring for a fresh pot of tea. Or perhaps you'd prefer a glass of homemade elderberry wine?"

The earl chuckled. "Elderberry? How original. My compliments, Mrs. Astell."

The warm regard mirrored in his eyes threatened to overset her. Margaret swiftly lowered her gaze. "You've managed to confuse me. Do you wish to take a glass of wine, or not?"

He awarded her a rakish grin. "Almost you tempt me. But, under the circumstances, I feel I must decline."

What circumstances? Margaret wondered.

"No doubt you are wondering the purpose of my visit," he observed.

Margaret sternly commanded her fluttering heart to calm down. Of all times for her mind to be a seething cauldron of fragmented thoughts, she lamented. "I must admit I'm curious. Pray enlighten me."

"Before we get into that, I beg you to believe I mean no personal slight. The truth is, I can't help but admire you, Mrs. Astell. So young and lovely to be raising five children alone."

Just what was all this flummery leading up to? Margaret asked herself. For certain, the toplofty Earl of Pardo hadn't come to court her. The daughter of a dealer in second-hand goods was unquestionably beneath his touch. Unless of course he had *carte blanche* in mind. A surge of indignation engulfed her. Earl or no, if he dared offer her a slip on the shoulder, she'd give him a tongue-lashing he'd never forget.

"I think it would be best if you came straight to the point."

"Very well. Not to mince words, I've come, Mrs. Astell, to inform you that I do not approve of my cousin dangling after your daughter. Not that she's not a pretty minx, for she is, but she won't do for Miles."

Margaret grappled with an almost overwhelming urge to slap the callous expression off the Earl of Pardo's face. To think only seconds ago, she'd thought he might be attracted to her, she fumed. More fool she!

"A viscount is obliged to look somewhat higher for a bride. I am sure, upon reflection, you will agree that I'm acting in his best interest."

"Why attempt to bully me, my lord? Why don't you take this up with your cousin? Or doesn't your opinion carry any weight with him?"

"Madam, you forget yourself. Of course he respects my opinion. At least he did till *your* daughter cast out lures."

"How dare you? Henrietta hasn't the least notion what lures are. Be assured I shall tell your cousin of your meddling in his concerns. He'll not thank you, I'll warrant."

"No, you're right on that head. But Miles is my heir. I shall do whatever is necessary until he comes to his senses. Come, be reasonable, Mrs. Astell," he coaxed softly. "Will you not train your daughter's sights a trifle lower?"

Margaret gathered the shreds of her wounded dignity about her and said quietly, "My lord, I believe you are making a great piece of work over Lord Stuart's many kindnesses to the Astell family as a whole. If that is so, this degrading interview was totally unnecessary."

Noting that he meant to interrupt, she checked him with her raised hand. "No, I shall have my say. Henrietta is not the least interested in being paraded before Society with the idea of catching a husband. She only agreed to make her come-out because I insisted."

Margaret lifted her chin. "However, it is my duty to see her comfortably settled. Thus, should it come to pass that their feelings are engaged, I don't plan to throw a rub in their way."

"Madam, I fear your underbred roots have surfaced," the earl said coldly. "Clearly, I'm wasting my time. I bid you good day."

As he turned on his heels, Margaret snapped, "Underbred indeed! Birthright is no guarantee of good breeding if you are any example. Without a doubt, you, sir, are the most conceited, pompous jackanapes I've ever met in my life — nobleman or no!"

The Earl of Pardo barely checked his stride, but as he crossed the threshold, he muttered, "Little spitfire."

The slamming of the front door proved to be the final straw to Margaret's overwrought sensibilities. Sinking into the generous folds of an upholstered chair, she burst into tears.

7

"Good morning, Lucian," called Lady Stuart from the top of the stairs.

The Earl of Pardo peered up at his aunt, debating the wisdom of awarding her a curt greeting and taking hasty leave as opposed to devoting a few minutes to pleasantries before going about his business. His sense of decorum won, and he moved to join her as she reached the foot of the stairs.

"Where are you off to so early? A ride on your charger?"

"No. I'm taking the phaeton." Twinges of guilt played havoc with his scruples, though his bland demeanor gave no hint of inner qualms. "I have an appointment at Whitehall."

"Then I won't keep you. Shall you be home this afternoon? The charming Astell ladies come to us today."

"Here? To St. James's Square?" He

raised one dark, disbelieving eyebrow.

"You'd think I'd invited the Princess of Wales, or some other unsuitable creature. Are you hinting you don't wish me to entertain the Astells? I realize this is your home and that I'm only a guest, but it never occurred to me you might disapprove of anyone I choose to entertain." Lady Stuart's face mirrored her perplexity. "Perhaps you'd be good enough to tell me why you object?"

"Object? Whyever should I?" the earl thundered. "The fact that your son is behaving like a besotted gudgeon over a chit whose grandfather was in trade stands as nothing in my book!"

A glimpse of his aunt's stricken face smote his conscience. He broke off his tirade, contenting himself with a furious scowl.

"Lucian," his aunt said, in a careful, reasonable tone of voice, "do you not think you could bring yourself to view their visit with a little less heat? Miles has his heart set on my becoming better acquainted with the Astells. Frankly, I, too, look forward to it. Margaret Astell is reputed to be a respectable widow, and her daughter, a pretty, well-behaved young miss. As a particular favor to me, will you not come and give them a fair chance?"

"See here, Aunt Min. You should be encouraging Miles to look elsewhere, rather than abetting his apparent wish to attach himself to a penniless young upstart."

"Fiddle faddle! Such a dust you are kicking up because Miss Astell is not plump in the pocket. Even if you should have a change of heart and get buckled, Miles is comfortably situated."

"Me marry? Perish the thought." His recent close scrape with the Countess of Chilsea invaded his mind, but he resolutely pushed the memory aside. "As heir to my title, Miles owes it to our distinguished forebears to pick a wife of more equal lineage."

"How pompous you sound. Be careful, nephew. You're in danger of becoming too starched up with family pride."

"Why shouldn't I be? We descend from a noble line."

"So we do, but an occasional infusion of sturdier yeoman stock would not go amiss. I am convinced constant inbreeding results in too many high-strung females and in gentlemen given to vile tempers and queer starts. Not to mention all the addlewits, squint eyes, receding chins, crooked teeth, sick headaches, and putrid breaths it produces."

The rich vein of irony inherent in his

aunt's feisty rebuttal surprised a crack of laughter from the earl.

"Enough, Aunt Min, enough. I cry craven." Eyes glittering with sardonic amusement, he added, "I must be off, else I'll be late."

"Judging by the tone of your remarks, I gather you don't wish to see the Astells," she stated coolly.

Up shot a supercilious eyebrow. Why bypass a perfect chance to catch the Astells in some vulgar lapse that might open Miles's eyes? "My dear Aunt Minerva, you couldn't be more mistaken. I shouldn't dream of not being on hand."

Three quarters of a hour later, the earl waited in a Spartanly appointed anteroom to be summoned by Viscount Palmerston. Lucian had just halted his restless pacing to pluck a bit of fluff off the sleeve of his morocco brown driving coat when a lackey entered to advise that he'd been deputized to escort him to the secretary at war's office.

Good old Harry, Lucian mused as he followed the lackey. Despite Viscount Palmerston's scholarly record at Cambridge, his more recent gallant attentions to the ladies had earned him the nickname of Lord Cupid. Still in all, no one doubted Palmerston's political star was destined to rise. Harry had only been five and twenty when Perceval had appointed him secretary at war, Lucian reflected. Now four years later, Palmerston was a seasoned veteran of both the War Office and Parliament where he was the MP representing his alma mater.

Ushered into the viscount's presence, the two men exchanged a handshake before Palmerston asked, "Something in the wind, Lucian?"

"Harry, I am in a deuced quandary. I need your help."

"Always happy to do what I can. Have a chair."

When both men were seated, Palmerston coaxed, "Now, what's your problem?"

"Concerns my cousin, Miles," Lucian admitted tersely. "I hate like the very devil to involve you, Harry, but I fear the consequences if I don't throw a spoke in his wheel."

"Your reticence does you credit, but if you want my help, you will have to be a trifle more forthcoming. Rest assured I never betray a trust."

"I know that, Harry, else I'd never dream of confiding in you. Not to beat about the bush, I think Miles contemplates forming a misalliance."

"Is that all?" Palmerston looked visibly relieved. "I shouldn't worry if I were you. As soon as Stuart acquires a little town bronze, he'll cease to behave like a lovesick puppy who's slipped his leash."

The earl frowned. "I wish I could share your optimism. I fear the attachment may be serious."

"Even so, Stuart strikes me as a fairly level-headed young officer. Why not approach him openly and state your objections?"

"I doubt he'd listen to me. Much more likely, he'd resent the unasked-for advice, and since he's of age I no longer have the authority to order him to stop seeing the troublesome chit."

"Bribe the wench to cry off," Palmerston suggested.

Lucian shook his head. "Such a ploy might work with a lightskirt, but the young lady's respectable enough, despite the fact that her late grandfather was in trade. Besides, I already tried to warn her mother against the match. She chose to ignore my advice."

Palmerston laughed. "Which didn't sit too well, I warrant."

"Just so," the earl drawled.

The secretary at war cleared his throat.

"Want to help of course. Thing is, I fail to see how I can."

"A forced separation will bring Miles to his senses. If you could arrange for his unit to be called up."

"I see what you're driving at. However, moving troops about is the Duke of York's bailiwick."

"I know that, Harry, but I thought I might persuade you to drop him a hint," the earl stated, rising to his feet. "Whatever you decide, I won't keep you any longer. I know you are busy."

"Dash it, Lucian, hang on for a minute. I'll do what you ask, if you insist. I just want it clearly understood that what you suggest is a drastic measure that, once set in motion, is irreversible. Are you certain you won't change your mind?"

"Absolutely not."

"Very well then. I'll have a word with the Royal Duke."

"I appreciate it, Harry. You will keep me informed?"

"Depend upon it. I'll be in touch as soon as I hear anything definite," Palmerston assured him.

Considerably later in the day, Lucian jaunted down the curved stairs inside his town house in better spirits than he'd enjoyed that morning. Determined to do his aunt proud, he'd exchanged riding breeches and Wellingtons for a dark blue coat of Bath superfine and narrow gray trousers. Rising to the occasion, his valet had even managed to fold his neckcloth into a commendable Mathematical, Lucian conceded as he entered the music room. Once inside, he ran a proprietorial eye over the handsome Adams ceiling and mantelpiece, commissioned by his grandfather, the 3rd Earl of Pardo. Next, he admired the Sevres china his dear departed mother had brought into the family as part of her dowry and gave a nod of approval to the sterling silver flatware and gleaming silver tea service that graced the lace cloth.

Lady Stuart joined him. Determined to make amends, he made her an elegant leg. "My apologies, ma'am, for my boorish behavior. You are free to invite the Astells to tea, or anyone else who happens to take your fancy."

"I daresay you climbed out of bed on the wrong side this morning."

"More than likely," he agreed meekly.

Shortly after making his peace with his aunt, the earl heard his cousin's voice. Seconds later, Miles entered with Margaret Astell on one arm and her daughter on the other.

While greeting his aunt's guests courteously, Lucian assessed their appearance, which admittedly he found faultless. Henrietta's dress was a lilac muslin with gauze sleeves sprinkled with tiny embroidered violets while Margaret bedazzled in a silk gown of delicate rose.

Though he did his best to keep a tight rein on his emotions, he was irritated that once again the matron's mature beauty made his heart pump faster. As soon as he could manage it, he maneuvered her toward a wall of French doors overlooking a formal garden. "Perhaps you would care to take a short stroll, Mrs. Astell?"

Margaret shot him a suspicious glance. "No, thank you. I prefer to spend my time in this charming room." Her eyes widened with pleasure as they came to rest on the pianoforte.

Noting her change of expression, he promptly led her to it. Gratified by her look of awe as she ran her fingers across the ivory keyboard, his own gaze lingered fondly on a delicate instrument built by Broadwood and Sons as he recalled his departed mama's deft touch.

"Are you musical, Mrs. Astell?"

"Not in the least. It is the grace of the piece I am so taken with. Sheraton, I believe."

"Correct. You admire furniture?"

"I do if its lines are pleasing and the wood of superior quality. Or if the embellishment is particularly cunning such as the Wedgwood medallions decorating this handsome pianoforte." Margaret smiled a trifle mischievously. " 'Tis an interest I inherited from my father. He was a secondhand dealer you know." Her chin tilted challengingly.

The earl was tempted to laugh at her attempt to goad him, but amusement swiftly gave way to a poignant surge of regret. When he'd called on her in Wimpole Street, his harsh tongue-lashing on that occasion had hurt her feelings. He deserved to be horsewhipped. "Mrs. Astell, I wish to apologize for my excessive rudeness the last time we met."

Margaret lowered her gaze. "I collect my own manners were not too nice on that occasion."

"Shall we cry *pax?* I don't think my aunt desires us to ruin her party by trading insults."

"I confess I shouldn't care for that either."

"A truce then?"

Margaret nodded her assent. Lucian caught a whiff of lilacs. Manfully, he resisted a mad impulse to gather her in his arms. An act he had absolutely no intention of pursuing, being neither a lecher nor a sapskull.

Fighting to regain his equilibrium, he seized upon the tea table, now abrim with refreshments, as an excuse to break up their *tête-à-tête*. Escorting her there, he grinned when he noticed Margaret eying the chairs with frank interest.

"Hepplewhites," he said.

"I know," she said dryly. "Their shield-backs interest me. They're a trifle unusual."

Once everyone was seated and sipping their tea, his aunt addressed Henrietta. "Do you still go to Hookham's? I've not run into you there lately."

For a minute, Henrietta looked ill-at-ease, but catching sight of the playful twinkle in Lady Stuart's blue eyes, she soon relaxed.

"Yes, ma'am. I exchange my books twice a week."

The earl arched an eyebrow. "You, like most young misses, are addicted to novels, I assume?"

"Indeed I am, sir. Toby and Ned prefer adventure stories."

"And you, Mrs. Astell? Do you have a preference?" Margaret shook her head. "To be frank, I prefer to sew."

"Mama is not much of a reader, my

lord," Henrietta confirmed. "Nor are my twin sisters. It's the boys and I who are prodigious readers."

Lady Stuart smiled. "I'm presently reading *Sense and Sensibility*. I recommend it highly."

"Who is the author, ma'am? Did you get it at Hookham's?"

"No. Miles presented the book to me as a gift. Where did you purchase it, dear?"

"Hatchard's in Bond Street."

Her ladyship turned back to Henrietta. "I should be happy to lend it to you when I finish it, Miss Astell. The author is at present unknown. The title page states 'by a lady.' "

"Then, she's following in Miss Burney's footsteps," Henrietta remarked.

Lucian judged it time he rejoined the conversation. "Miss Burney's married name is Madam d'Arblay. Her husband's a French royalist. It's my understanding they've been trapped on the Continent ever since the resumption of the hostilities."

"If that's the case, we can only hope the d'Arblays steer clear of Napoleon," Miles observed.

"I pray that they do." Henrietta beamed a smile at her handsome young suitor, before fixing awestruck eyes upon the earl. "Lord

Pardo, you certainly know a great deal about one of my favorite authors."

Lucian shrugged off the compliment, though he could not help feeling pleased that for once Miss Astell wasn't regarding him with hostile eyes.

"You write, too, do you not, Miss Astell? Ned says you are very good," Miles volunteered, a little put out by the attention Henrietta had bestowed on his cousin.

An electrifying silence greeted the viscount's statement. The earl was startled to catch a flicker of anger in the pretty widow's face, whereas her daughter's reflected abject misery. Lucian frowned, mystified by their reaction to Miles's civil inquiry.

When Margaret finally spoke, she seemed to weigh each word carefully, "I collect you refer to the journal my daughter keeps, Lord Stuart."

"Of course I am, ma'am," the exceedingly relieved viscount hastened to agree.

Lady Stuart, who seemed anxious to alleviate an undercurrent of uneasiness, quickly added, "I kept a journal when I first came to London. It helped me to adjust to the strangeness I felt as a result of being taken straight from the schoolroom and thrust into Society." She bestowed an understanding smile upon Margaret. "A perfectly unexceptional pastime for a green girl in her first Season, I assure you, ma'am."

Margaret visibly relaxed. The earl took pains to make himself agreeable, despite the fact that his mind was busy trying to discover the reason the conversation had upset her.

Was it possible that Henrietta Astell was a blue-stocking? Lucian asked himself. He looked with sympathy on Margaret. Should it get out that the troublesome minx was an intellectual, her mother had about as much chance as an icicle in hell of finding an eligible nobleman to take her bookish daughter off her hands.

Henrietta smiled at her hostess. "When you are finished, ma'am, I should very much like to read the novel you spoke of so highly."

"I shall be happy to send it along with my son the instant I've turned the last page."

A quarter of an hour later, Margaret stated firmly they must go. Once Miles had left to take them home in his berlin, Lucian sought out his Aunt Minerva.

"What did I tell you, Lucian? I knew if you could be persuaded to climb down off your high horse, you'd like them both."

Naturally, he wouldn't dream of

spoiling his aunt's pleasure. Besides, having struck the telling blow, he could afford to be generous.

"Indeed, Aunt Min, I'm glad you invited them. Truth be told, I cannot think when I've spent a more interesting afternoon."

8

In the elegant ballroom of Devonshire House the last note of music died. Henrietta, attired in a silk gown of *bleu celeste* with square neck and slashed short sleeves, smiled dreamily up at her companion. How handsome Miles looks in evening dress, she reflected. All his clothes fit well, neither too tight nor too baggy, and she was grateful he didn't favor the garish colors and extreme fashions of a pink of the *ton*.

"It's devilishly warm in here. Let's saunter to the punch bowl and refresh ourselves," Miles suggested.

Henrietta's heart beat a little faster as she placed her arm in his. It was her first ball, and no matter how many times she pinched herself, she still felt as exhilarated as Fanny Burney's Evelina. Naturally Miles was the noble Lord Orville. In a happy daze, she made no protest. After going to the buffet table to procure two glasses of lemonade, he guided her into a quiet alcove.

"Henrietta, there's something I must tell you," Miles announced in a strained tone.

Henrietta shivered. Something in his voice awakened a premonition that everything was about to change. She stared into his face, seeking reassurance. Instead, the determined set of his jaw and the somber cast of his features raised goosebumps on her bare arms. What could be troubling Miles? Was his starched-up cousin still pressuring him to break off his courtship? After taking tea in St. James's Square, Henrietta had begun to hope that the proud earl would have a change of heart. No such thing! Obviously, he still felt the Astells were beneath his heir's notice.

Oh the unfairness of it. If only she had a dowry, Henrietta lamented. Not that it would signify. The Earl of Pardo was so puffed up in his own conceit, he'd never countenance a match with someone whose grandfather had been in trade. Odious man. Resentment flickered in her eyes. Swiftly, she lowered her gaze to her dainty white kid slippers.

Miles's pointed cough recaptured her attention. Henrietta peered up at him quizzically.

"My regiment's been ordered to join Wellington on the Peninsula. I leave at first light."

Henrietta's head reeled. Dear God. How foolish of her to imagine her only enemy was the earl. If that were the case, at least she'd have stood a chance of winning Miles's regard. But the British army was something else again. It was too big, too faceless to fight. An overwhelming sense of panic assailed her. She was going to lose Miles — perhaps only for a time — perhaps forever.

Miles gently raised her chin with his forefinger. "Henrietta, did you hear me?"

"Y-yes. You've been ordered to join Wellington?" The pain was unbearable. Henrietta fought to contain it. "It's just such a . . . shock. I know you're a commissioned officer, but I never dreamed you'd be sent to Spain."

"I'm surprised myself. My unit has been held in reserve to defend home soil in the event Boney should attempt to cross the Channel. That danger has dwindled so markedly ever since he launched his Russian campaign, I'd all but given up hope of ever seeing any action." The smile he awarded Henrietta was endearingly boyish.

"Oh, Miles. You wish to go, don't you?"

How dare he look so eager. Didn't he realize he could be killed? If that should happen, her heart would break.

Miles sobered. "Of course, I don't wish to leave you. But the more countries Bonaparte gobbles up, the more he craves. England is not safe while he rules." His eyes held a fervent expression. "Wellington has crossed into Spain. My unit is needed to augment his forces."

"I see." To her own ears, her voice seemed faint . . . far off. She loved him so much. A hard knot of misery gnawed at the pit of her stomach.

Henrietta felt as if someone had yanked a rug out from beneath her. Parties and balls would seem flat without him. But this was hardly the time to feel sorry for herself. It was Miles who would be in constant danger. She paled at the daunting thought. "I . . . that is, all the Astells shall miss you, Miles." A lump gathering at the base of her throat made it difficult to get the words out.

The viscount's gaze grew tender. "I shall miss you, too, Henrietta. Will you write to me?"

"I . . . I . . . it wouldn't be proper."

"I had not considered that stricture," he

admitted after a lengthy pause. "Promise me you'll call on my mother. With only my cousin to rely on, she'll be lonely."

"But of course. I'm quite fond of her you know. Besides, she will be able to tell me how you go on."

"She's fond of you, too, Henrietta. Now, much as I hate to, I must return you to your mother's keeping."

Miles escorted her to Mrs. Astell, and her new partner waited to claim her hand for the next set. As she danced, the room seemed to take on an aura of unreality. Disoriented, she had no idea what her partner said to her during the pauses in their patterned steps, much less what she distractedly replied. The frivolity of the occasion seemed such a mockery considering the grim fact she might never see Miles again. Unsure of how long she could keep up a pretense of gaiety, Henrietta gazed beseechingly up at candles glistening in magnificent crystal chandeliers, willing the interminable set to end.

At last it did. Henrietta murmured an excuse, then bolted before her partner could lead her back to Margaret.

Gathering her skirt in both hands to ensure she wouldn't trip, she scurried up a gracefully curved staircase and into the ladies' retiring room. Overset, she searched her reticule, removing a dainty handkerchief which she used to blot away tears just beginning to trickle down her cheeks.

The dressing table mirror reflected a face marked by distress and agitation. Miles was going to Spain. There was a strong probability he'd see action. How distressing to learn such dire news in the midst of a ball. Not that she blamed him. Miles hadn't been given much notice. He'd had to tell her tonight or not at all. Henrietta dabbed at the corners of her eyes and daintily wiped her nose. What a pity Miles must go away just when she discovered how deeply she cared for him. But she mustn't give way to despair. Miles would come back. He must!

She permitted herself one more sniff of self-pity, before tilting her nose ceilingward and sailing from the room. At the foot of the stairs, she smoothed the skirt of her gown and began to ease her way back to the ballroom.

As she passed a slightly ajar door, raised voices wafting from within piqued her curiosity. Peeping inside, she was surprised to see the Earl of Pardo and the Countess of Chilsea embroiled in an argument. Henrietta couldn't help but admire Lady

Chilsea's vivid pink gown, done up in shimmering satin and set off by diamonds circling her neck and dripping from one wrist.

The countess thrust her hand in front of the earl's face. "Thank you for the bracelet, Lucian," she said coldly.

"A parting gift, Henny. I am glad you like it."

Even to Henrietta's innocent ears, it was obvious that the earl had given his former *inamorata* her *congé*. It was also quite clear he did not respect her. And no wonder. The countess, so proud of being highborn, had the morals of a courtesan.

He cast a wintry smile that, although it didn't appear to discompose the countess one whit, sent icy chills coursing along Henrietta's spine. I should die if Miles ever looked down his nose at me like that, she thought. Thank goodness, Miles was blessed with a sweeter nature than his cousin.

The countess's shrill voice shattered Henrietta's concentration.

"I feel compelled to drop a hint in your ear, Lucian. Little Henrietta seems to have engaged your cousin's regard. I should have thought you'd too much pride to permit such an obvious misalliance," the countess said snidely.

Henrietta clamped her lips together tightly so she wouldn't cry out in protest of the searing pain squeezing her heart.

"My dear Countess, what a poor opinion you have of my wits. I hesitate to boast, but I've friends in high places willing to do me an occasional favor. The instant I noticed my calf-sick cousin dangling after the penniless chit, I set a plan in motion guaranteed to end the affair."

"Miles is of age, is he not? Do enlighten me, Lucian. Pray how do you propose to break the attachment?"

"That, Countess, is my little secret," the earl gloated. "Rest assured the gossips will soon need a new topic to take the place of the unsuitable match between my heir and your cit niece."

"Splendid. I'm heartily sick of meeting Henrietta and Margaret at every fashionable affair. I imagine they'll retire to the country once the romance ends. And good riddance."

The earl recoiled. "By God, Henny, you're a vindictive bitch."

"Stuff! Who are you to cast stones? When it comes to snobbery you take the palm." The countess slapped shut a *chinoiserie* fan. "I shan't detain you any longer, Lucian. I know you are anxious to return to the ballroom so you can resume flirting with my sister-in-law. Are you considering setting her up as your mistress?"

"That, my lady, is none of your business. This conversation grows tedious. Do excuse me."

Not having the smallest wish to be discovered eavesdropping, Henrietta skittered noiselessly down the corridor. Entering the ballroom, she lost no time reaching her mother's side.

"There you are, dearest. I've been concerned."

Henrietta was pleased to see the worried look vanish from Margaret's face. Her thick chestnut curls were arranged in a soft coronet, secured by a narrow strip of forest green velvet. Indeed, Mama looked so lovely, so serene, Henrietta had to catch her breath.

Indignation flared. If the earl ever dared make Mama a disrespectable offer, by heaven, Henrietta vowed to get even. Quite unbidden, an idea tumbled into her head. A curious smile played on her lips. Her hazel eyes glittered. Ah, sweet revenge.

"Such a grimace," Miles observed as he rejoined Margaret and her daughter. "Who's put your back up, Miss Astell?" he teased.

Henrietta's expression softened. Dearest Miles. So kind. So considerate. He always addressed her formally unless they were quite alone and could safely revert to first names. Now as he straightened from an elegant bow, she saw a hint of mischief in his gaze.

"Our dance, is it not?"

"But, Miles, this is a waltz."

"I know, but I've just come from a heart-to-heart chat with Lady Jersey. Since I leave for Plymouth in the morning, she graciously grants you permission."

Henrietta broke into a smile. "That's wonderful, Miles. I shall adore waltzing with you."

"Come along then. I don't want to waste a single bar of music."

Henrietta soon became a part of a whirling band of gracefully spinning couples. How she loved being held in Miles's arms. The feel of his strong, firm hand pressing lightly at the small of her back made every nerve in her body tingle. While she thoroughly enjoyed the delicious sensations, she was also embarrassed by her growing awareness of his manly physique. Still, even though her cheeks burned hotly, she wished it were possible to savor the intimacy of the moment forever. In the next instant, her spirits plummeted as she realized Miles might not ever hold her so close again. Fighting tears, she bit her trembling lower lip.

All too soon the waltz ended. Miles said softly, "How about a stroll in the garden before I take you in to supper?"

"I should like that above all things," she confessed, her eyes glistening with unshed tears.

Outside, Henrietta gazed up at an inky sky aglitter with twinkling stars. The night air on her bare arms felt refreshingly cool. A gentle breeze caused the leaves to rustle in the tall trees. A perfect May evening.

Miles paused before a stone bench where he bade her be seated. Though Henrietta expected him to sit beside her, he began to pace up and down. Something was cutting up his peace. Henrietta waited patiently for him to confide in her. Abruptly Miles came to a dead stop.

"Henrietta, I must speak. My deep affection for you is too overpowering to keep bottled up inside me. I know it is selfish of me to attempt to fix your interest when I must absent myself for heaven only knows how long, but . . . do you think you could come to care for me enough to marry me?"

An expression of joy lit Henrietta's countenance, but was swiftly vanquished by one of despondency.

"Lucky for you, I'm not so unscrupulous as to snap up your offer. You know as well as I do that my origins are too humble to suit a man who will someday be an earl. Why I don't even have a dowry. I'm deeply honored, but I must refuse."

"Why you silly little widgeon," he cried fondly. "I don't care a fig for your pedigree or your purse."

Henrietta frowned. "Your cousin will never approve the match. I should not like to think I was the cause of your being disinherited."

"I collect you are under the mistaken impression that if we marry, I shall lose my chance at the title?"

"Won't you?"

"No. I'm next line whether my cousin approves of my chosen bride or not. The only way Lucian can cut me out is if he marries and begets his own heir. Which he's welcome to do for all the difference it makes to me."

"Are you saying you don't care about the title?"

"I already have a title and a comfortable income. Viscount suits me just fine." He regarded her closely. "It is a yes?"

"Yes!" Henrietta cried.

Watching a bedazzling smile spread slowly across his beloved's face, a surge of exhilaration shot through the viscount. He wasted no time in pulling Henrietta to her feet and to her rightful place against his hard, lean chest. At first he practiced restraint, but then, spurred by her shy, tentative response, Miles rained kisses on her eyelids, her cheekbones, her sweetly shaped mouth.

Minutes later, he reluctantly checked the mounting intensity of his emotions and backed away, while at the same time, steadying Henrietta's swaying body with a gentle, but firm, pressure on her upper arms until she regained her balance.

"My dear, I fear I must take you in to supper this instant, else our prolonged absence is sure to set tongues wagging."

"Indeed, you are right," a still-shaken Henrietta responded shyly. "I daresay Mama will be up in the boughs if we don't show ourselves at once."

As he escorted her back inside, Miles said in an exuberant tone of voice, "Now that we are betrothed, we may write to each other. I confess I did not think I could join Wellington's army with the proper equanimity without the comfort of knowing we may exchange letters." An anxious look filled his lean face. "You will write regularly, won't you?"

"Oh, yes, I promise. Indeed, I shall look forward to it. As Ned let slip, I am never so content as when I am scribbling away."

A glint of amusement enlivened the viscount's features. "So I've been given to understand," he said dryly.

All through supper, he frequently fixed his gaze upon Henrietta in a desperate attempt to commit her sweet face to memory. As for Henrietta, she deliberately avoided thinking about their imminent separation. Picking at her food, she told herself sternly she'd have plenty of time to wallow in self-pity once Miles had gone. Instead, she repictured the dance they'd shared in mind's eye. Her expression grew dreamy. If she lived to be a hundred, she knew she'd never forget dancing the waltz for the first time while being held in his arms.

Several hours later, the Earl of Pardo stumbled a bit unsteadily as he wove across the marble-floored anteroom of his imposing town house in St. James's Square.

After the ball, he'd looked in at White's, where, with an uncharacteristic recklessness, he'd lost several hundred pounds playing faro, before returning home to find Miles waiting to speak to him.

"Lucian, I know it's deuced late, but as I must leave at the crack of dawn, it's imperative I have a word with you."

Squelching a weary sigh, the earl gestured toward his study. "No need to rouse the entire household. Let us repair to the book room."

Upon entering, the earl staggered to a wing chair and sank wearily into it.

"Out with it, Miles, else dawn will break before you've had your say."

"Lucian, I am the happiest of men. Wish me joy. Miss Astell has consented to marry me. I confess I'm up in the alts."

"So I see," the Earl of Pardo said glumly.

Damnation! His scheme had misfired, veering down a path he had not foreseen. A peculiar expression dominated his sardonic features. With the air of a man who'd mistook vinegar for wine, he said, "Allow me to tender my congratulations."

As his cousin prattled happily, Lucian forced himself to come to terms with the result of his meddling. But for his machinations, Miles might not have proposed to Henrietta Astell. At least not so prematurely. Perhaps never. Hoist on his own petard, the earl silently acknowledged.

"I've written out an announcement that I wish to appear in the *Morning Post.* If you will be so good as to see to it, cousin?"

The earl roused himself from his brown study to say tentatively, "I'll abide by your decision, of course, but I wonder if it would not be wise to keep your engagement a secret for a time? This is Miss Astell's first taste of Society, I collect, and she is entitled to enjoy all the admiring compliments she can garner. I don't wish to play the voice of gloom, but in the event you don't return, it would make it easier for her to pick up the threads of her life after a time. What do you think, Miles?"

A brooding expression settled upon the viscount's features. After a lengthy pause, he said with obvious reluctance, "I hadn't thought of it in that light. Perhaps it would be better if our betrothal is known only amongst the family circle whilst I'm abroad. I shouldn't like to spoil her pleasure in her first Season. And though I don't contemplate it, it's pointless to deny I could die on the Peninsula. If that should happen, I should like to think that Henrietta would soon recover her zest for life. But what shall I do in regard to this announcement? I told her I would arrange to have it posted before I left."

Slightly encouraged that he might gain this small victory from his otherwise ignoble defeat, the earl said graciously, "Perhaps you will trust me to call upon the Astells and explain the delicacy of the matter? If they agree, the engagement will remain a secret known only to the immediate family until you return. On the other hand, should they feel something is havey-cavey about the change in plan, I'll soothe things over and hand carry the announcement to the *Post*."

"Yes, that seems best. I thank you for your trouble, Lucian. At least our betrothal means that Henrietta and I may write to each other. As long as that is possible, I don't care a button whether the world at large knows we are engaged or not."

"It's no trouble, Miles. I trust being engaged will encourage you not to indulge in needless risks. Don't worry about Miss Astell. I shall see that she comes to no harm in your absence."

"I appreciate it. Though Henrietta doesn't want for sense, you know."

"On the contrary. She's a needle-witted young miss if ever I saw one," the earl agreed ruefully.

"You'll take care of my mother, too, will you not?"

"Aunt Min? How can you ask? I'm near as fond of her as you are." On that note, they shook hands and parted.

Mounting the stairs, the earl ruminated unhappily. What had possessed him to poke his nose into his cousin's affairs? Even Palmerston had tried to warn him. Why hadn't he listened? Lucian flinched as he faced the unpalatable truth. When Margaret Astell had dared to defy him, his overweening pride had goaded him to outmaneuver her. Sickened by the unflattering self-revelation, the Earl of Pardo gave an inward shudder.

In his zeal to avoid a misalliance, he'd never stopped to consider the consequences. No wonder he'd lingered at White's this evening. Subconsciously, he hadn't wanted to face what he'd done. Lucian hung his head, thoroughly ashamed of himself. He was unworthy of his title. Unworthy of the great family whose name he bore.

Dismissing his valet, the earl's mind continued to roil. Devil a bit. The strings he'd pulled behind the scenes left a bitter taste in his mouth. For if his cousin died on the battlefield, Lucian would have to live with the fact that he'd had a hand in it. Filled with remorse, he solemnly vowed to behave more responsibly in future.

Much as he hated to admit it, Aunt Min was right. He was too damned puffed up with family pride by half. But, if at all possible, he was determined to change. It was the only way he could regain his self-respect.

9

The next day, after seeing his heir off at first light, Lucian spent the morning with his private secretary catching up on his correspondence. However, in the afternoon he climbed into his pearl gray barouche with his family crest emblazoned on the side door.

The coachman cracked a whip in the air. The elegant high steppers set off at a brisk trot.

Unhappily for Lucian's peace of mind, as they neared Upper Wimpole, he was assaulted with a fresh round of remorse. For despite his intention to turn over a new leaf, the fact remained that, due to his scheming, Miles might be killed on the Peninsula. Should such a tragedy occur, the earl was certain he'd never be able to look Aunt Minerva in the eye again.

However, it was pointless to dwell on what couldn't be changed. What he could do was look after the Astells, Henrietta in particular, as promised.

When the barouche drew to a stop, the earl shook off his misgivings. Alighting, he sauntered up the steps and lifted the knocker. Jonas responded.

The earl handed him his hickory walking stick and his top hat. "Are the ladies receiving callers?"

"Wait here, my lord, I'll inquire."

The receiving chamber was sparsely furnished, though in good taste, Lucian decided while cooling his heels. He was relieved when Jonas returned before he had a chance to grow truly restless.

"Mrs. Astell and her companion, Miss Potts, will receive you in the sitting room."

Lucian raised one black, questioning brow. "And Miss Astell?"

Jonas gave a deep sigh. "No doubt, she will join you presently. This way, my lord."

Ensconced in the attic, Henrietta's pen flew across the page of her journal. Whenever she paused to rest her hand the sad fact that Miles was bound for Spain lowered her spirits. Consequently, even though her fingers were beginning to cramp, she pressed on, because only when she concentrated her full attention on the book she was writing did she manage to momentarily forget how hurt and dejected she felt that Miles had been obliged to desert her side. Providentially, she'd wakened at daybreak with the entire next chapter of her novel clear in her mind. All morning, her hand had itched to write everything down. Henrietta gave a rueful sigh. Trust Mama to have other ideas. She'd insisted Henrietta try on two new gowns so Miss Potts could pin up their hems.

Thus, it was only after a hurried noon meal that Henrietta had been able to make good her escape. Thank heaven, she hadn't forgotten anything important, she thought as she painstakingly recorded the unfolding scene.

Leonardo seized Pamela's hand and declaimed passionately, "Rest assured I shall return to press my suite as swiftly as I can."

"Go this instant, my brave one, lest you miss the tide. Whilst you are gone, I shall take care to elude the coils of that cruel tyrant, the Count di Moro."

"Farewell, my heart!" exclaimed Leonardo as he leapt into the gondola.

The boat had merged with the horizon before Pamela could bear to tear herself away. By the time she sighted the abbey in the distance, she felt excessively weary. But knowing she'd soon be safely within its walls, she drew in a deep breath, with the intention of releasing it in a long sigh of relief. Unhappily, at the exact instant she inhaled, the wicked Count di Moro stepped directly in front of her. With a startled cry, Pamela turned to run back the way she'd come. However, her hope of slipping from di Moro's grasp was doomed to failure, for the wily count's henchmen had already surrounded her. Only seconds later, Pamela found herself overpowered.

She flinched as the count's fiendish laughter defiled the airwaves. Pamela longed to cover her ears. Alas, her hands were bound. Then, one of the henchmen gave her a shove. She fell in a crumpled heap at the feet of the wicked Count di Moro.

"At last, my proud beauty, you are mine to command."

"Never!" Pamela shouted passionately.

Count di Moro peered down his aristocratic nose at her in that odiously condescending manner she thoroughly detested.

"A few days imprisoned in the castle dungeon will no doubt turn you up sweet," he proclaimed with haughty disdain.

Pamela trembled. She was afraid of the dark, terrified of locked rooms. If only Leonardo . . .

A faint whistle accompanied by belabored wheezes broke Henrietta's concentration. Irritated by the interruption, she peered down the steep, murky stairwell.

Espying Jonas, his pudgy face beet red from his exertions, she called, "No need to climb any farther. What do you want?"

Speaking haltingly, he said, "The Earl of Pardo is paying a call, miss. Madam desires you to change your gown before you join them."

"Fiddle!" Henrietta exclaimed. She'd reached a crucial point in her story and was sorely tempted to beg off.

"Mrs. Astell sounded urgent, miss."

"Oh, very well. Tell her I'll join them directly."

As Jonas trudged down the stairs, Henrietta flew to the small secretary she used to write her novel. As she closed the journal and hid it away, a mischievous smile enlivened her face. Perhaps she could turn an unwelcome social obligation to her advantage. A few more of the haughty earl's mannerisms would help flesh out her fictional villain.

One flight below, in her bedchamber, Henrietta washed her ink-stained hands and donned a sprig muslin, its high neckline enhanced by a stand-up ruffle.

As she entered the sitting room, the earl greeted her with a smile. "I'm pleased to see you are determined to keep up your spirits, Miss Astell."

Though he sounded sincere, Henrietta was put instantly on guard. Somehow or other he'd managed to have Miles's regiment called up. Of that she was certain. How fortunate she had chanced to overhear his conversation with the countess. If she'd had to judge him by his present manners alone, she might never have believed the earl was such a master of deceit and duplicity.

Once Henrietta had settled into one of Mama's prized Hepplewhite chairs and the earl had resumed his seat, Margaret picked up a letter resting on an end table and handed it to her. "Dearest, it's from Miles. Lord Pardo was kind enough to deliver it to you."

"I'm obliged to you, sir." She accepted the letter but made no move to open it.

A speaking look passed between Margaret and the earl. Henrietta frowned, at once suspicious as to what had transpired before she'd joined them. Knowing how impossible it was for Enid Potts to keep a secret, Henrietta regarded her steadily. Disconcerted, the spinster nervously averted her gaze to the white India cotton shirt she was sewing for Toby.

Slightly piqued, Henrietta said with

acerbity, "I collect all of you have already been apprised of the contents."

The earl pointedly cleared his throat. "While I did not read your letter, Miles did confide in me before he left. In turn, I confess I did relate some of the fine points to your mother, Miss Astell. I apologize if this offends you. Miles asked me to put a notice in the *Morning Post* announcing your engagement. This I shall certainly hasten to do, if it's still your wish after you've heard me out. I advised my cousin that since he must absent himself from London for an extended period, it might be wise to postpone a formal announcement, keeping the betrothal known only amongst the immediate family until he returns."

Henrietta clenched the letter in her hand. Such colossal cheek! Not content with removing his cousin from the scene, the wily earl wished to scotch any official notice of their engagement.

Before she could think of a biting rejoinder, the earl continued. "I took the liberty of pointing out to Miles that it was selfish of him to expect you to forgo any of the pleasures of your first Season, especially as it is bound to be dull for you with him away. Perhaps you would care to read Miles's message and then let me know how you feel in regard to this matter."

Henrietta slowly broke the wafer and unfolded the thin sheet of vellum. "Excuse me," she murmured with absent politeness before reading the words her betrothed had penned only hours before.

To be perfectly honest, she shrank from a formal announcement, particularly without Miles on scene to lend his support. However, it went against the grain to give in meekly to the earl. Who knew what nefarious scheme he might hatch next, spurred on by the success of his campaign to separate her and Miles?

"It's not as if you and Miles may not exchange letters, dearest," Margaret remarked gently.

In truth, that was all Henrietta cared about. As long as they might write to each other without raising any eyebrows, and as long as she knew she had Miles's love and regard, she didn't care whether society in general knew of the betrothal. In point of fact, it might be a dead bore, occasioning all sorts of social obligations that she would just as soon avoid. Especially now, when she was feverishly involved with pulling all the facets of her first work of fiction into a cohesive whole.

Henrietta forced a sweet, compliant

smile to her lips. "My lord, I must own I agree. I would much prefer a postponement of the announcement until Miles returns. I would imagine there is a great deal of fuss that accompanies such an announcement here in town."

"Miss Astell, I commend your good sense. As head of my family, I beg you and your mother to feel free to apply to me for aid in any matter that may occasion a male's protection during Miles's absence. I am sure my aunt would be most pleased if you ladies will call upon her as frequently as convenient in St. James's Square. It will help her keep up her spirits."

"Yes, of course, my lord. Mama and I shall be happy to pay our respects to such a fine lady."

Surging to his feet, the earl addressed Margaret. "I hope I may have the pleasure of calling again soon."

Brown eyes twinkling, Margaret nodded. "Certainly you may, Lord Pardo. It's almost tea time. Will you not join us?"

"Thank you, no. I've another engagement." His dark eyes lit with curiosity as they flitted to the parlor archway where the Astell twins paused, their brother, Toby, just behind.

"If you can spare a minute, my lord, I

should like to present my younger children."

"My pleasure, ma'am."

Smiling encouragement, Margaret bade Hannah and Hester and Toby to enter. Once they had, she made them known to the Earl of Pardo. As the girls made their curtsies and Toby bowed, Margaret ran a critical eye over her twin daughters' white batiste dresses, belted with azure blue silk sashes chosen to match their eyes. A wave of gratitude swelled in her breast. Thank goodness they'd taken time to brush the tangles from their hair and slip into the demure gowns.

Even luckier, to her mind, was the fact that the earl's taciturn demeanor served to curb their normally boisterous spirits, while his gallantry rendered them tongue-tied.

"My eldest son, Ned, has returned to Harrow," Margaret explained, when she'd completed the introductions.

"Ah yes, Ned. Cousin Charles's closest friend at school, I believe. Miles is also deuced fond of Ned. Though naturally he's not as taken with him as he is with your eldest daughter, ma'am." Amusement glittered in the earl's eyes.

Mercifully — in Margaret's view — before her three youngest became easier in his company, the earl had left.

As the pearl gray barouche bowled over cobblestones, the earl's mood turned pensive. He'd more or less steeled himself for an unpleasant scene once he'd apprised the Astells of the fact that he'd persuaded Miles to postpone a formal announcement of the betrothal. He'd been so certain that Margaret would rip up at him, and when she had not, he'd fully expected that Henrietta would. She'd declined to do so also, leaving him puzzled.

The younger Astells had been a pleasant surprise. All in all, a handsome family. He had to hand it to Margaret. How she'd managed to raise five children and still look like a schoolgirl fresh from the country was beyond him. Smiling, he recounted every detail of her lovely face and luminous brown eyes. Her taste was impeccable — both in her dress and in the way she'd decorated the sitting room. He'd been piqued when he'd called before, but on this occasion he'd taken time to admire the flocked wallpaper and the Hepplewhite chairs. And Miss Potts, no beauty in anyone's copy book, added an air of respectability to the household.

The earl's face darkened. He'd tried to

skirt the main point, but long habit of ruthless self-appraisal forced him to meet the unvarnished truth head-on. The Astells might lack a long line of noble ancestors — on Margaret's side — but they were not likely to put the Pardo-Stuarts to the blush. He ought not to have acted so precipitately.

However, what was done was done. All he could do now was pray his cousin came home from the war raging on the Peninsula safe and sound.

At least, he'd been sincere when he'd offered to lend his protection and aid to the Astells whenever necessary during Miles's absence. Not that any small service he might perform could ever make up for his inexcusable conduct. Damn his stiff-necked pride. If only he'd had sense enough not to meddle. But it was too late for regret on that head. All he could do was persist in his struggle to change his future behavior. No doubt, his conscience would continue to tweak him at odd times, cutting up his peace. If so, it was only what he deserved.

With a supreme effort he called a halt to his mental wandering and struggled to infuse some cheer into his dashed spirits. Leaning out of the barouche window, he called, "Set me down at White's if you please."

After Jonas cleared away the remains of their tea, Margaret picked up a nightgown she was edging with a fine strip of lace, but she soon thrust it back into her workbasket. Enid had gone on a errand in Bond Street, taking the twins along. At first Margaret had been grateful when Henrietta had suggested taking Toby with her to Hookham's so he could personally exchange his books.

Margaret's expression was wry. Quite often she longed for a little peace and quiet. For once her wish had been granted, but was she content? No, indeed. She was so used to being surrounded by her family that she actually felt bereft with them gone from home, though no doubt she'd soon rue the fact that she hadn't taken time to enjoy her rare solitude.

A smile broke upon Margaret's face. She'd been indoors too much of late. She'd go for a walk. With a pleased trill of laughter, she went to fetch her bonnet.

Twenty minutes later, she'd covered the distance separating Upper Wimpole from Regent's Park and was strolling along Park Crescent, Luke trailing behind her for propriety's sake.

For once she was free to enjoy herself, and she was quite determined she would. She paused to admire a bed of tulips, thinking what a pity it was that they had such a short blooming season. Her countenance sobered as she likened her own blossoming into womanhood. Like the tulips, it had been all too brief. One minute she was going to *ton* parties and balls; the next she was married. John Astell had been too impatient to allow her to enjoy a full Season. At the time, Margaret had naïvely believed it was because he loved her too much to wait, but she'd soon learned to regret her foolish assumption. No such thing. Her husband hadn't loved her at all. His reason for rushing her to the altar was that he couldn't wait to get his hands on her generous dowry.

Margaret winced. Fool that she was, she'd actually spent years bowing to John's petty demands. Far too late, she'd realized all she'd earned by her cheerful compliance was her husband's contempt. But it was folly to dwell on the unhappy past. John had been dead over a year. She was finally free to please herself, and the weather was too fine to let unhappy memories spoil her pleasure.

Margaret smiled as she recalled how well her progeny had behaved when introduced to the Earl of Pardo. Her pulses quickened as she pictured him in mind's eye as he'd stepped into her sitting room wearing checkered trousers with a brown frock coat and a gold silk waistcoat. How she'd longed to feel the varied texture of each item with her fingers. Whatever would he have thought of her, had she yielded to temptation? Blushing, she admonished herself. Idiot! He'd assume you were either mad or odiously forward.

But, my oh my, how his tailor must love to dress such a well-formed body, Margaret mused. Even when the hot color in her cheeks had faded, her mind continued to ramble unchecked. What would it be like to be held in his arms? Instinctively, she knew the answer. Pure heaven. A pleasurable shiver played tag with her spine.

Margaret drew to a sudden halt. She was being beyond permission foolish, she reprimanded herself sternly. The Earl of Pardo wasn't the least interested in her. He was only being kind when he'd paid a call on her family. As for herself, she was being overly fanciful when she'd imagined the warm regard in his eyes as he lingered over her hand.

With a dejected sigh, Margaret set off for home.

10

Three months later, on a crisp September morning, the Earl of Pardo tried to contain his impatience as he waited for Margaret Astell to join him in her sitting room. Much to his chagrin, the pretty widow was fast becoming an obsession. Initially, he'd been convinced he'd only to absent himself from town during August and September and his preoccupation would quickly wane. However, despite a lengthy tour of his estates — beginning with Chesterwood, where he'd invited his cousin, Charles, and Ned Astell to spend their summer holiday — he hadn't been able to cure himself of his infatuation. On the contrary, the taking creature had been constantly on his mind.

Even more upsetting, he'd had a devilish time sleeping. Consumed with desire, night after night he'd tossed and turned. Worst of all, whenever he did manage to drift off,

Margaret haunted his dreams. Thus, asleep or awake, she obsessed him. The earl gave a sardonic chuckle. Talk about a lovesick sapskull. This morning he'd wakened at dawn refreshed from the best night's sleep he'd had in weeks. So what had he done? His involuntary peal of laughter held a derisive note. Immediately after breakfast, he'd proceeded to pace up and down in a fever of impatience, half convinced he'd go mad before the hour hand of the clock reached eleven. And now, against his better judgment, here he was at Upper Wimpole paying her a morning call.

"Lord Pardo, what a surprise! I understood from Lady Stuart, you're not due back in town for another two weeks."

Rising as she entered, his eyes brimmed with mischief. "Since I finished my stint of estate business early, I decided to rush back to town to set up a flirtation with my favorite widow."

Margaret sent him a speaking look, then slowly spread her fan and began to wave it in a spuriously seductive manner. "La, sir, you flatter me."

"Keep batting those big brown eyes at me like that, and I'll carry you off to my lair before the cat can lick its ear," he warned gruffly.

Blushing becomingly, Margaret politely invited him to sit down. When he'd complied, she assumed the chair opposite and asked, "How does Ned go on? I trust he hasn't plagued you to death?"

"No, indeed, ma'am. His health was stout when I stopped off at Chesterwood on my way to town. My gamekeeper informed me both he and Charles have become dedicated fishermen." Lucian grinned. "The boys appear to have wormed their way into Cook's good graces. At least she professed herself pleased to deal with their daily catch."

Margaret's answering smile was fleeting. "Ned does tend to go overboard with his latest enthusiasm. I hope it won't be necessary to restock your streams once he and Charles return to Harrow."

Lucian laughed. "I don't begrudge them a single trout. It's a small price to pay to see Charles so content."

"Even so, it was kind of you to invite Ned to accompany him to your family seat. Used to living in the country, I am convinced Ned would have been miserable if he'd had to spend his holiday here in London."

"Just so, ma'am." Lucian frowned. It had crossed his mind to invite all the Astells to

Chesterwood at the conclusion of the London Season. Unfortunately, Aunt Min, who was a very poor traveler, had decided to remain in town. Naturally, without his aunt in residence, it wouldn't have done to invite Margaret and her brood.

His countenance cleared. "Ned and Charles are due to arrive by week's end. I felt a few days in the bosom of their families were called for before they begin the autumn term."

"How thoughtful of you to be sure."

"Spare me from expressions of gratitude, I beg you. Where is Miss Potts today?"

"Enid's in her room, nursing a cold."

"Pity." The earl did his best to sound sincere; however, it was hard to hide his delight in having Margaret to himself for once. "And Henrietta?" he asked.

Margaret smiled. "She'll be sorry to miss your visit. She's taken my three youngest children for a walk."

"Good. There are one or two things I want to discuss with you in strict confidence."

"You intrigue me," Margaret admitted. "Pray continue."

Her smile was so enchanting, Lucian couldn't stop himself from returning it. However, it simply would not do to allow himself to become entangled in an emotional morass. His smile faded with his renewed determination to stick to business.

"Firstly, I wish to thank you and your daughter for paying frequent calls on my aunt in my absence."

"Not at all. I assure you Henrietta and I enjoy our visits quite as much as Lady Stuart evidently does."

"Nevertheless, I appreciate it. I also called to invite you and your daughter to accompany Aunt Min and myself to a musical evening at the Russian Embassy next Tuesday."

"We'd be delighted."

"Furthermore, I've a mind to give a ball in Henrietta's honor."

Margaret looked stunned. "Surely there's no need for such an extravagant gesture."

"I'm afraid I must insist. Late October would be ideal. By then the little Season will be in full swing."

"Lord Pardo, I beg you to reconsider. Without Miles here, I am persuaded Henrietta will dislike so much fuss."

Undaunted, the earl radiated confidence. "Ah, but that's the beauty of my scheme. If Wellington runs true to form, he'll order his troops to billet down in their winter quarters from October through December. Ergo, Miles stands an excellent chance of being granted a short leave. Henrietta's ball would be the perfect occasion to announce their engagement."

Margaret stared at him, her uncertainty plain to see. "Is it possible you've become reconciled to the match?"

The Earl of Pardo responded with a hearty chuckle. "Reconciled is too tame a description, ma'am. High time I confess to a complete change of heart."

She treated him to an incredulous look. "Really? You amaze me."

"In that event, I'm glad I broached the matter early. It will give you time to grow accustomed to my about-face. Now I must take my leave, for I fear I've stayed a trifle longer than is strictly proper."

Bending, Lucian bestowed a quick kiss on the back of her hand. Catching a tantalizing whiff of lilacs, he found himself reluctant to break contact. As if mesmerized, he deliberately turned her hand over and brushed his lips across her slender wrist. His heartbeat slammed against his rib cage when Margaret reacted with a long sigh that seemed like music to his straining ears.

Straightening, his eyes swept her lovely face. Her cheeks were suffused with a rosy blush, and he noted with heady satisfaction that the tiny pulse embedded in the hollow of her throat was beating frantically.

Common sense resurfaced. Good God! What was he thinking of? If he didn't watch out he'd find himself trapped in a compromising position with this enchanting Circe, his only honorable option an offer of marriage. Lucian gently released Margaret's hand and backed out of the room. Even so, the scent of lilacs lingered, and a century seemed to pass before he found himself inside his moving carriage bound for St. James's Square.

Quelling a shudder occasioned by his close scrape, Lucian leaned out the window and ordered the coachman, "Spring 'em!"

On a balmy autumn evening, inside the Russian Embassy, Henrietta sighed as the final perfectly pitched note of the renowned Italian soprano, Signora Mininni, held the audience — comprised of the cream of the London *ton* — enthralled.

Then, scattered cries of "Encore! Encore!" accompanied by a flurry of clapping, broke the spell. However, the guest soloist of Countess Lieven's musical soiree proved impervious to demands that she subject her precious vocal chords to any additional strain. Obviously agitated by the audience's inability to empathize, the short, dumpy woman exited in a burst of volatile Italian totally unintelligible to the English ear.

While Henrietta watched the unfolding drama with rapt interest, Countess Lieven, wife of the Russian ambassador appointed to the Court of St. James's, stepped quickly into the void created by the singer's disgruntled departure. With the graceful raising of her arms, the ambassadress silenced the murmur of voices and restless stirring of those seated upon the unpadded, straight-backed chairs.

"My dear friends, the selections sung by Signora Mininni conclude the musical program. However, I hope you will linger to converse and to partake of the cold collation spread out on the dining-room table."

She had began to edge away from the stage area of the vast room, when a masculine voice stayed her retreat. "Shame on you, Countess. You've not performed yet."

"Very true," a second deep voice agreed. "How can you think of fobbing off your guests so shabbily?"

Their hostess attempted to demur, but this only spurred on a general clamor that she play something for them on the pianoforte. Finally, her expression a mixture of gratification and consternation, Countess Lieven laughingly gave in.

"La, you do me too much honor. However, as you insist, I shall be happy to oblige you after a short recess."

Much scraping of chairs ensued as the major portion of the audience climbed to its feet.

"Does she play well, ma'am?" Henrietta asked Lady Stuart. "Extremely well, my dear. Indeed, Countess Lieven has many talents. She's fluent in four languages and a renowned hostess on a par with the Ladies Holland, Cowper, and Granville. Moreover, she's astute enough to keep on friendly terms with all three."

"A female paragon to be sure," Henrietta responded, tongue in cheek. She studied the Russian woman's tall, angular figure, fascinated by her too-pronounced features that ruled out beauty by a mere fraction.

Lady Stuart's ice blue eyes twinkled. "Be that as it may, I don't think the countess is our cup of tea. Though undeniably attractive and too clever by half, I must tell you, she detests reading."

"How very odd. Dear me, I believe she's headed in our direction."

"So she is," Lady Stuart agreed. "I don't

145

believe I recognize her escort."

Unfortunately, Henrietta did. Her pulses raced as a series of alarms rang in her ears. For, unless her eyes deceived her, Charles Lowndes, her Fleet Street publisher — the last person on earth she ever expected to run into at such a fashionable affair — had offered the ambassadress his arm and was guiding her on a course calculated to ensure their paths would cross.

Gracious, what a coil! An agitated frown disturbed Henrietta's brow. To think she'd been so pleased when Lowndes had sent word he was going into a second printing as the book was selling so briskly. However, her pleasure had faded when the publisher had begun to press her to discard her anonymity and allow if not her true name at least her *nom de plume* to appear on the cover of the novel. But never mind raking up past bones of contention. For the moment, she'd be grateful if Lowndes didn't betray their connection.

Henrietta took a deep breath. She dared not dwell on the consequences should the earl ever learn she'd borrowed his mannerisms and gestures to make her villain lifelike. Lord save her! If he ever found out, he'd wring her neck.

Henrietta frowned. When she'd delivered

146

her finished novel to Lowndes the last week in May, she never dreamed he'd manage to have the book in print a scant month later. Nor had she dreamed it would be in such demand. Needless to add, even in her most fanciful nightmare, she'd never dreamed that she and her publisher would ever move in the same social circle, thus placing her reputation in dire jeopardy. Henrietta shuddered to think what reprisals Countess Lieven would enact, should she learn that one of her guests was the authoress of a work of fiction. Her hostess was one of the patronesses of Almack's. At the very least she'd withdraw Henrietta's voucher.

Fleetingly, Henrietta considered quitting the room, but such behavior would seem very odd to Lady Stuart. No, she couldn't run. She must brazen it out.

Though her insides were shaking like blancmange, somehow or other she managed to appear composed as their hostess and her escort joined their party. While Henrietta struggled to call her scattered wits to order, Countess Lieven nodded to acknowledge Lady Stuart, before smiling graciously at Margaret and her daughter.

"I am so pleased to meet the Astell ladies, whom, I understand, are often in your company of late, my lord." Smiling coyly, the countess rapped Lucian's knuckles lightly with her fan. "But la, I'm neglecting my friend. Allow me to acquaint you with the publisher, Charles Lowndes. It's my guess you've a bone to pick with him." She cast the earl a sly look.

Obviously nonplused, but cognizant of the innuendo inherent in the countess's remark, Lord Pardo said bluntly, "I haven't the vaguest notion what you are hinting at. Pray enlighten me, Dorothea."

"Really, Lucian, I never suspected you were a slowtop. Surely you're aware that all the ton is agog trying to guess who may be the author of *Pamela's Folly*?"

A pensive scowl wrinkled his brow. "Now that you bring the matter to my attention, I do seem to recall some mention of it at White's."

The countess smiled sweetly. "According to an impeccable source, wagers as to who the author is have been recorded in the betting book. I understand they're laying odds that the villain of the piece is modeled after you."

" 'Pon my honor, ma'am, I had no idea!" the suddenly alarmed publisher interjected.

Henrietta felt a flutter of panic in her

stomach. Suppose Lowndes unwittingly gave her away?

"Devil a bit! Dorothea, are you hoaxing me?" the earl queried sharply.

"Certainly not! Why do you suppose I went to the trouble to pry this gentleman loose from his printing press in Fleet Street? He's all the rage amongst the *ton,* though I'm the first hostess to lure him into the social whirl. If you choose not to believe me, feel free to consult Lady Cowper or Lady Jersey. They'll be quick to tell you why everyone's been staring at you so particularly all evening. Depend upon it, Lucian. The villain is you to the shade."

Henrietta swayed a little. She was forced to grip the back of a nearby chair to keep from toppling. Feeling the color drain from her cheeks, she cast a feverish glance at Margaret. The look of polite interest on her mother's face came as a decided relief. How upset Mama would be, should she ever find out that the daughter she trusted had broken her promise.

Henrietta gripped the back of the chair so hard her knuckles bled white. It would never do to fall into a dead faint. To do so would draw unwelcome attention, something she very much wished to avoid. Fortunately, she noted, the earl appeared to be wholly preoccupied by the unexpected attack on his honor and seemed to take scant notice of her agitation.

"I shall consult with Emily and Sally at the earliest opportunity, I promise you, Dorothea."

Henrietta was appalled to see the light of battle in the earl's eyes as he focused upon Mr. Lowndes. "Tell me, sir, how do you countenance publishing novels anonymously? To my mind, it's cowardly."

Charles Lowndes looked amazed. "My lord, I beg leave to inform you, it's a time-honored practice that has never been seriously called into question. There are many legitimate reasons an author may not wish to reveal his identity. None, as far as I can see, dishonorable, much less cowardly."

"The deuce take you, sir. Assuming the gossips are correct, without a name how can I call to account the dastard who's blackened my character?"

Henrietta's sense of foreboding burgeoned as she noticed that the earl's vehemence affected the printer adversely. Lowndes's lean face paled, and he nervously shuffled his feet as if afraid that should the earl fail to discover the author of the novel in question, he might decide to persecute the publisher instead.

When the earl made a mirthless chuckle, it was clear to Henrietta he'd correctly interpreted the printer's concern for his own skin. "Don't worry, sir. I know you didn't write it. If, indeed, the novel does contain a character modeled after me, it follows the author has to be a member of the *ton*."

"You refine too much on it, my lord," said Lowndes. "The current prattle is mere conjecture. *Pamela's Folly* is fiction pure and simple."

Lord Pardo frowned. "I should be inclined to concur if the prittle-prattles hadn't met with such marked success in spreading the slander abroad. I'll get to the bottom of it. Of that you can be sure."

Noting the earl's face was again darkening, Countess Lieven assumed command. "Lucian, would you be so kind as to escort me to the pianoforte and help me select a piece?" She smiled flirtatiously.

Succumbing to her flattery, the earl issued his hostess a charming smile. "My pleasure, Dorothea. I'll even turn the pages while you play."

"You are too kind."

As Countess Lieven and the Earl of Pardo moved off, Henrietta, who felt she'd been holding a pent-up breath for an eon, released it in a heartfelt sigh of relief. But her elation was short-lived. Sensing his interested gaze, Henrietta shot a glance at Charles Lowndes. Despite his benevolent expression, her heart sank. For unless she was very much mistaken, the reprieve she'd won was only temporary.

11

Several days later, the morning sun found Henrietta seated upon the sofa, which was covered in cranberry satin, leafing through the latest copy of *La Belle Assembleé* when Jonas entered to announce the Earl of Pardo.

Margaret set aside her needlepoint and glanced into the mirror on the wall. Apparently satisfied she was looking her best, she instructed the butler to show their guest in. At any other time, Henrietta might have looked upon her mother's primping with amusement, but her sense of humor had been at low ebb ever since she'd unexpectedly encountered her publisher at Countess Lieven's.

Consequently, it took all of her determination to assume a pleasant mien as Lord Pardo strode into the room. Clad in a gray linen frock coat and houndstooth trousers, he was obviously in high gig as he made his bows to Miss Potts, dearest Mama, and herself. Indeed, lulled by his exuberance into a false sense of security, Henrietta found her gloomy state of mind fading and was about to issue a tentative smile when he removed the book tucked under one arm and set it upon the occasional table next to the sofa. One glimpse at the gold lettering on its spine was all it took to cause Henrietta's spirits to plummet.

"I've brought you ladies a copy of *Pamela's Folly*," he announced with a complacent smile.

"Did you indeed?" Margaret cried. "Wherever did you find it? My own efforts have been so frustrating. The lending library has a long list of names before it will be our turn, and Hatchard's has sold out."

The earl laughed. "Had I known you were so anxious to read it, ma'am, I should have shown up on your doorstep the instant Aunt Min turned the last page. I brought it today because I know your daughter shares my aunt's penchant for reading. But, perhaps I should offer it to you first?"

A delicate flush effused Margaret's face. "I confess the discussion at Countess Lieven's has piqued my curiosity."

Lord Pardo appealed to Henrietta. "How shall I resolve my quandary? Can you bear to wait until your mother is done?"

Henrietta was honestly perplexed by his affability. She'd assumed he'd climb up on his high ropes the instant he got his hands on her novel. Unless of course he hadn't bothered to read it. A distinct possibility, she admitted. More than likely he'd fly into a rage the second he did.

"Dearest, the earl asked you a question," said Margaret.

Henrietta blushed. "I beg your pardon, Lord Pardo. You were saying?"

"I asked if you'd mind letting your mother read *Pamela's Folly* before you do."

"I've no objection, my lord."

What else could she say without appearing uncivil? thought Henrietta. Fortunately for her peace of mind, his lordship transferred his attention to Margaret. "Thanks to your daughter's generosity, you may begin your perusal the minute I leave."

"I'm obliged to you, sir." A quizzical look displaced Margaret's warm smile. "Did Lady Stuart enjoy it?"

"Aunt Min pronounced it to be 'top of the trees.'"

Henrietta eyed him searchingly. "Have you read it, sir?"

"I scanned it," he admitted, after a lengthy pause.

On tenterhooks, Henrietta steeled herself to ask, "What did you think of it?"

His demeanor grew decided haughty. "I fear my taste doesn't run to melodrama, but then I'm not overly fond of romantic fiction."

Henrietta burned with resentment of his condescending assessment. However, she resolutely pressed on. "What of the villain? Did you see any resemblance to yourself?"

Margaret frowned at her daughter. "Henrietta. Such a rude question. Apologize at once."

"Forgive my want of tact, my lord. I fear I let my curiosity rule my tongue."

"No need to be so hard on the minx, ma'am. I took no offense."

Margaret responded to the earl's smile with a speaking glance, then shyly lowered her gaze. Observing the interplay, Henrietta wished she had time to ponder the significance of what she'd seen, but Lord Pardo was speaking to her again and Mama would really be upset if she didn't pay attention.

"To reply to your question, Miss Astell, the allegation that the villain is patterned after me is rubbish. There are superficial resemblances, of course. Both of us are titled noblemen, for instance. However, the count is an arrogant tyrant. Nothing like me at all."

Amazing! The starched-up earl didn't recognize himself. Henrietta stifled a nervous giggle. Laughter at this juncture would definitely not be the thing.

Upon reflection, she concluded that his lack of recognition wasn't as remarkable at it seemed at first glance. He simply didn't see himself as she did. And to be scrupulously fair, she'd exaggerated his weak points, particularly his overweening pride and his arrogance.

With the air of a man who rarely questioned his own judgment, his lordship ventured coolly, "In my opinion, the only reason the unfounded rumor was taken up by the tattlebaskets is because — what with Parliament in recess — there is precious little grist for the gossip mill."

"A tempest in a teacup?" asked Margaret.

The earl's mouth twitched. "Yes, ma'am. But enough on that head. I came expressly to discuss the arrangements for the ball I'm giving in St. James's Square to introduce Henrietta to some of our relations and particular friends. Aunt Min is quite taken with the idea." He shifted his gaze to Henrietta. "You were not present when I first broached the subject to your mother. I trust you have no objection?"

"It is very generous of you to suggest it, sir. But could we not postpone it until Miles can be present? In his last letter, he said it's impossible to get leave."

The earl cast her a sympathetic glance. "When I first proposed an October ball, I had high hopes my cousin could attend. But Wellington has got the French on the run. I make no doubt Nosey's determined to pour on the pressure, which puts paid to the possibility of Miles attending. I realize a ball in your honor would be more enjoyable with your betrothed present. Just the same, we cannot wait any longer. One of the reasons the gossips are so busy blackening my character is because the *ton* doesn't understand the nature of my friendship with the Astell family. However, if during the ball, I discreetly hint to a few of our particular friends and relations that you and Miles are betrothed, I feel certain it will put a period to the gossip."

Henrietta tried her best to squelch a resurgence of guilt. Although she still nursed a grudge toward the earl for engineering Miles's transfer to the Peninsula, she was forced to admit the nobleman had gone out of his way to look after the Astells in his cousin's absence. And how had she repaid his many kindnesses? The answer made her wince. By making him the villain in her Gothic novel, she'd exposed him to public ridicule.

"Naturally, I shall be pleased to do what I can to help scotch the rumors," Henrietta assured him, her repentant mood easing a little as she recalled his disparaging remarks in regard to her novel.

"It is decided then," he proclaimed, before changing the subject. "You mentioned you've a letter from Miles? How is the cawker?"

Henrietta blushed. "He's fine, sir."

"Excellent." With that, the earl rose to take his leave. Deftly, he captured Margaret's hand, obviously resolved to linger over his farewell as long as possible.

Taking advantage of their mutual absorption in each other, Henrietta scooped the book off the occasional table and jammed it behind the sofa cushions. Then, as unobtrusively as possible, she rose and moved to the hearth.

Enid Potts witnessed Henrietta's strange behavior, but pretended she hadn't. Knowing her situation to be precarious, she kept her tiny, ferret eyes trained determinedly upon the new evening gown she was trimming.

Once the earl left, Margaret glanced at the empty tabletop. "Gracious, what happened to the novel Lord Pardo brought?"

Henrietta fixed her gaze upon the same spot, feigning amazement. "Perhaps he took it with him without realizing it."

Margaret shook her head. "I'd have noticed. Besides, why should he do that?"

"I've no idea. But he must have done. It could hardly have vanished into thin air."

Used to years of self-effacement, Miss Potts debated the wisdom of holding her tongue as she continued to make dainty finishing stitches. The only sign of inner agitation was the fact that her pursed lips tightened a fraction. Whatever should she do? No question she owed Margaret a great deal. However, while Henrietta might have an odd kick to her gallop, Enid did not think the girl's action had been motivated by a selfish wish to read the novel first. Why then had she hidden it? In a state of wretched indecision, Enid wavered. Coming between mother and daughter placed her personal comfort at risk.

With a sigh, she put her sewing aside and approached the sofa. "Perhaps it's been misplaced. Let me have a look."

Henrietta gave a guilty start. The mere thought of having her deplorable duplicity exposed was enough to make her blanch. Sick at heart, she realized the seamstress must have seen her hide the book. For how else would she know just where to look?

"Here it is, Margaret," cried Miss Potts. "It must have slid off the table and got stuck behind a cushion."

Straightening, she handed the book to her friend.

Margaret looked puzzled. "How very odd. You were seated on the couch, Henrietta. Did you not notice?"

"No, Mama," she lied glibly.

Enid Potts threw her a censorious look. Henrietta was overcome with remorse. Never in her life had she told so many lies. Where would it all end? Her face burned with shame. Not only had she broken her word to her mother, the money she'd earned as a result weighed heavily on her conscience.

Henrietta's pulses drummed a harsh staccato against her temples. The last time she'd visited Barclay's, she'd discovered her bank account had swelled to nearly two hundred pounds. Mama could certainly put the money she'd earned to good use.

Yet, there was no way to tell her without confessing the whole.

A discreet clearing of a throat directed Henrietta's gaze to the room's entrance. Grateful for the interruption, she said with false brightness, "Yes, Jonas?"

"A Mr. Charles Lowndes has come calling, miss."

Henrietta gave a violent start, but made a quick recovery. "Has he indeed?"

What could her publisher be thinking of? He ought to know better than to call upon her in Upper Wimpole. His effrontery was most disturbing. Perturbed, she looked to her mother for guidance.

"I suppose there can be no harm in seeing what he wants," Margaret remarked. "Show him in, Jonas."

No doubt, she reflected, he'd been much taken with Henrietta at Countess Lieven's. It wouldn't do to encourage his attentions, however. For not only were Henrietta's affections already attached to Miles, but if the publisher found out Henrietta was a scribbler, no telling where a little encouragement from that quarter might lead.

Charles Lowndes strode purposely into the room to make proper bows to all three ladies before addressing Margaret. "Ma'am, I wonder if you'd be so kind as to

162

allow me to take Miss Astell for a drive in Regent's Park this fine autumn morning?"

Margaret vacillated. On one hand, Henrietta could do with a bit of fresh air. She was too much indoors since Miles's departure. No doubt she missed their daily excursions to Hyde Park during the fashionable hour. Yet Margaret had only met Mr. Lowndes at the Russian Embassy several evenings before and knew nothing of his background.

Noting her hesitation, the publisher hastily amended the invitation. "It may be a bit of a squeeze, ma'am, but if either you or Miss Potts cares to accompany us, you are most welcome."

"Very kind of you, sir, but Miss Potts and I are much too busy this morning. However, if Henrietta . . ." She sought her daughter's eye in order to discover her wishes.

"A drive would be capital," Henrietta exclaimed, resolving to use the time to discourage her publisher's pretensions. "Excuse me, sir. I'll go fetch my bonnet."

Once they reached the park, Lowndes favored Henrietta with an appraising glance. "I hope you won't take my calling upon you at home amiss. It was urgent that I speak with you."

"Ours is a business arrangement, sir. Could you not have written me in care of my bank as you did when you wished to inform me that you were bringing out a second edition?"

"What I have to say is best said in person. But first, how do you wish to receive the bonus I promised?"

"Deposit the funds due me into my bank account as usual. It won't do for us to be seen together often. If the scandalmongers find out who I am, I'm dished. So, if you please, what is the purpose of paying me a call?"

The printer responded in a bantering tone. "For all you know, Miss Astell, I may have developed a partiality for you and mean to pay my addresses."

"I sincerely doubt it. I'm sure your shop keeps you much too busy to be dancing attendance on a dowerless girl."

"Dowerless, but talented," he corrected playfully.

When Henrietta didn't respond to his raillery with so much as a flicker of a smile, the publisher's face sobered. "I collect I'm too far below your touch to interest you?"

"No such thing. My affections are already fixed."

He looked thunderstruck by this piece of news, but manfully pulled himself together. "It seems I must wish you happy, Miss Astell. Did I meet your intended at Countess Lieven's?"

"No. Miles is on the Peninsula with Wellington. But I must ask you to say nothing of my betrothal. It is not generally known."

"I see. What with your young man out of the country, I begin to understand how you found time to write a novel. Which reminds me, as your first work of fiction has proved so popular, I hope I can persuade you to write another. I'd be willing to pay double for it."

"Never again. Why if Mama ever finds out what I've done, she'll expire of shame. Pray, sir, if we've concluded our business, kindly return me to Upper Wimpole. I don't wish to appear ungracious, but I must ask you not to call on me at home in future. Should it be necessary to consult me, contract me through my bank as arranged."

"As you wish, Miss Astell. But I hope you will reconsider. I'd give most anything for another novel that would sell as briskly as your first, 'pon my soul I would."

Henrietta opened her mouth, meaning to saying something dampening, but before she could speak, Lowndes said, "Mull over my offer. Being a scribbler is nothing to be ashamed of."

"It's not writing in general I am ashamed of. It's the word portrait I sketched of the Earl of Pardo. I deeply regret patterning one of my characters after him."

"No need to fly into a pet. Lord Pardo hasn't a glimmer of suspicion that you wrote *Pamela's Folly.*"

"Not yet, he doesn't," came Henrietta's grim rejoinder.

Lowndes continued to try and ease her guilt-ridden conscience as the carriage rolled toward Upper Wimpole. However, nothing he said succeeded in lightening her morose mood.

What if Lowndes decided to pressure her to write a second novel by threatening to inform the earl of her identity? she pondered. The very thought sent a chill through her bones. Far, far worse, what would Miles think of her if he ever found out? He might cease to love her once he knew all. If she lost Miles's regard, her heart would shrivel to a cold, dead stone.

Lowndes handed her down from his carriage and escorted her to the door. While they waited for Jonas to respond to his knock, he said, "Please reconsider my offer. It would be a shame to scotch the budding career of such a talented authoress."

"Do give over, sir," Henrietta pleaded. "If someone overhears you, my goose is cooked."

As Jonas closed the front door behind her, Henrietta frowned. Actually, even if Lowndes ceased to pester her, the jig was up. How stupid of her to include a detailed description of Grandpapa's dining-room table in her book. Mama would be sure to recognize it.

Henrietta gave a deep sigh. Conceding that her mother would soon learn of her treachery, she prayed fervently no one else would. No question, Mama would be vexed. However, Henrietta doubted she'd be anxious to broadcast her daughter's disgraceful conduct. Thus, it was entirely possible no one else would learn of the wicked revenge she'd taken on Lord Pardo to pay him back for sending Miles into danger. Thank goodness. Because, if the earl ever found out, there'd be the devil to pay.

12

As the days passed, though involved in the details of staging a ball, Lucian began to entertain doubts. Though he still clung to the belief that the anonymous author of *Pamela's Folly* had not patterned the villain after himself, none of his peers held that opinion. Wherever he went, to his clubs, to Gentleman Jackson's, to take the air in Hyde Park, or to various social functions, members of the *ton* would stare — and very oddly. Entering a full room unexpectedly, he was all too often chagrined when a disquieting hush fell, followed at once by the disconcerting onslaught of chatter that somehow rang a false note in his ear.

By now, if the rumor had been spun out of thin air, it should have died. When it didn't, he decided further steps were necessary.

Accordingly, a few days later, the earl regarded the book room's Adam mantelpiece, hands locked behind his back. He turned as the door flew open and his butler announced, "Wilkins, sir," then ushered in a man, short of stature and clad in a bowler hat and a rumpled tweed overcoat.

As the door closed after the retreating butler, Lord Pardo impatiently motioned Wilkins to sit. Prompt to take the hint, the man perched gingerly on the edge of his seat, his close-set eyes furtively scanning the floor-to-ceiling shelves crammed with leather-bound books.

Stern faced, his lordship said, "I take it you're the Bow Street Runner I requested?"

"Aye, guvner, I be Wilkins, sent by old Sampson Wright hisself."

Belatedly noting the earl's pointed glare, he whipped off his bowler and set it on the end table next to his chair. Then, as if determined not to be further intimidated by the nobleman's disconcerting stare, Wilkins whisked out a well-worn Occurrence Notebook from an inside pocket of his overcoat. His pudgy, nondescript features assumed an official mien as he peered up at the tall nobleman.

"Now, sir, let's get down to business. Who's the flash cove you wish me to find?"

"Who, indeed? I haven't the foggiest.

169

But I mean to find out. That's why I've engaged you."

"I need to know all the particulars before I can get my dabblers on the criminal. What's his lay?"

"His what?"

"What's he done? Be he a footpad, a pickpocket, a highwayman, a cutthroat?"

"None of those," the earl admitted. "The dastard's impugned my good name. I must learn who he is so I may call him out if he's a gentleman, or if not, call him to account."

"Impugned your name, m'lord. Be that a criminal offense?"

The earl's dark eyes withered Wilkins with a frigid stare. "Of course it is. It's libel."

Wilkins canceled a shrug and took care to school his pudgy features to a professional blandness. Sampson Wright had confided the Earl of Pardo was too demmed starchy about his highborn rank, but for all of that was "a right 'un."

Since the Runner's reputation in Bow Street owed much to his dogged persistence, the officer of the law pushed on. "Libel is it? And how did the offense come about, m'lord?"

"Why the blackguard's a scribbler who's

had the curst effrontery to put me in a novel he wrote."

"A scribbler?" the Runner asked dubiously.

"Yes. While I've no idea who'd dare serve me such a turn, he must be of my class. For how else would he know so much about how Society goes on?"

Wilkins pounced on the promising scrap of concrete information. "Mayhap, if you wuz to search your cockloft, you'll recollect the scribblers amongst your set."

"Don't you think I already have?" Lucian ripped up at the Runner. "I regret to say I'm at a standstill. I cannot think of anybody who both bears me a grudge and is a scribbler to boot."

"Guvner, it be me duty to warn you with so little to go on, it'll take some doing to find out who the bloke is."

"I think not. I've neglected to tell you the man's publisher is Charles Lowndes, who maintains a printshop at 76 Fleet Street."

Understanding oiled the cogs inside the Bow Street Runner's mind. Brightening visibly, Wilkins cried, "That's the ticket, guv! Now we be getting somewheres."

He began to write furiously in his Occurrence Notebook. "I'll lurk about Fleet and nab this libeler-mort and haul him off before the Bow Street magistrate before the cat can lick its ear."

The earl frowned. "No, I don't wish you to lay a hand on him. All I wish you to do is discover who he is. Are we clear on that head?"

Wilkins gave a reluctant nod, his mind busy considering whether he was duty-bound to warn his lordship about taking the law into his own hands. A quick glance at the earl's grim features and set jaw sufficed to convince the Runner that any sermonizing on the legal point would be most unwise.

"I get your drift, guvner," Wilkins assured the nobleman, before setting off to begin work on his latest case.

Margaret turned the last page of *Pamela's Folly* and closed the book with a snap. Her brown eyes flashed. The fact that the novel had disappeared from the table immediately after the earl's visit was no accident. No doubt Enid had seen Henrietta hide it behind the sofa cushions, but hadn't liked to tattle. With the advantage of hindsight, Margaret could well understand why her daughter hadn't wanted her to read it. While the setting of the novel was purported to be Italy, the silly child had furnished the villain's castle with pieces taken straight out of Tobias Hicks's manor house. Margaret could only hope none of their neighbors in the country would remark on the resemblance. Why the troublesome chit had even had the gall to describe her grandfather's black mahogany dining-room table right down to the nicks in one of the legs, put there by Ned's hound puppy, subsequently banished to the kennels in disgrace.

Margaret grimaced. How the nicks got there was beside the point. Her eldest daughter's perfidy was the bone of contention. How dare she disobey me? After she'd promised, too. A searing pain encircled Margaret's heart. Never in her life could she remember being so hurt. But then, she'd trusted her daughter. More fool she.

Margaret felt like crying. But playing the watering pot was out of the question. Tonight was Henrietta's ball.

A soft rap on the bedchamber door jarred her from her gloomy ennui. Clutching Henrietta's work of fiction to her breast, she called, "Come in."

Entering, Enid Potts's tiny black eyes went straight to the book Margaret held.

"Is that the one the earl brought?"

"Yes," she admitted, wishing she'd had the forethought to hide the volume before bidding Enid to enter. "Gracious! How late is it?"

"That's why I came. If you still wish to bathe, you've just time before dinner."

"I most certainly do."

Enid's thin lips twisted into a half-smile. "Your hot water's waiting on the stove. I'll go belowstairs and tell Luke and Jonas to lug up the cans and the bath."

The instant Margaret was alone, a frown reasserted itself on her brow. She itched to give her eldest the trimming she deserved. Yet, at the moment, she was too up in the boughs concerning Henrietta's outrageous behavior to broach the subject. In the white heat of anger, she might say something that cut too close to the bone.

Besides, it would be very unwise to raise the issue on the eve of the ball. After the pains the Earl of Pardo and Lady Stuart had taken, it would be grossly unfair for Henrietta to turn up at St. James's Square with red-rimmed eyes. A second knock on her bedchamber door broke her reverie. With a sigh of resignation, Margaret laid the book upon her dressing table and called permission to enter.

Waiting in the reception line inside the town house in St. James's Square, Margaret lifted her chin a fraction. She was determined to enjoy herself. Therefore, when, an hour into the ball, the earl requested she stand up with him for a waltz, she readily assented.

"You're in looks tonight, Mrs. Astell," the earl remarked as he led her toward the room's center. "Your gown is ravishing. I vow there must be a new mantua-maker who has set up shop."

"I make all our gowns. With Enid's help of course."

"Are you hoaxing me? The workmanship is exquisite."

A faint pink tinted her cheeks as Margaret conceded with airy nonchalance, "I enjoy fashioning our gowns, and even the prodigious needlework most of the time." Mischief enlivened her soft brown eyes. "As for style, I've been told that I inherited Papa's unerring eye."

The earl's black eyes twinkled. "You seek to provoke me? Shame on you, ma'am. Granted Tobias Hicks's method of amassing a fortune was a trifle . . . unusual, I'm too long in tooth to be shocked.

175

Besides, I understand he retired from trade to play the unexceptional country squire for several years before his death, did he not?"

"You are well informed, sir," she replied coolly.

"Only if the subject piques my interest. Speaking of which, I beg leave to tell you that I'm not your only admirer. I've caught many envious glances as we walked to the dance floor."

"Do you take me for a flat, my lord? It doesn't necessarily follow that the looks I garner are admiring ones. Besides, why assume it's me they're staring at? It could just as well be you. I make no doubt they are wondering why you are dancing with a matron, well past her first bloom, when you might have honored one of their infinitely more eligible daughters."

The earl lifted a supercilious eyebrow. "Oh? If they don't know by now that I've not the least fondness for insipid young misses, it's hardly my fault. However, I think you mistake the matter, ma'am. To my mind, the glances were all admiration and directed toward you. And no wonder! I vow there's not a female in the room wearing a gown that'd hold a candle to yours."

Margaret laughed. "Since you refuse to yield the point, I collect I must give over."

"Good. I see the musicians are finally set to play."

The waltz began at a slow pace. Following the earl's masterful lead, Margaret could not help an inward glow as a result of his praise of her skill with the needle. Though she hoped she wasn't in danger of becoming too puffed up with conceit, she did honestly feel her shimmering eggshell satin gown set off her complexion and dark chestnut hair. As the tempo of the waltz quickened, the enormous chandeliers suspended from a Venetian ceiling put on a dazzling light show, since hundreds of dangling teardrops of cut crystal reflected the glow from embedded candles.

Whirling in time with the music, the glittering combination of candlelight and crystal served as a magical pendant, charming Margaret free from all worldly cares. As she danced, the years seemed to melt away until she felt as giddy as a young girl attending her first ball. So carried away was she, that while she knew perfectly well that the earl was not handsome, his features appeared so to her. Devilishly handsome. Her heart fluttered as she inspected his attire. Clad in black evening coat and knee breeches, patent slippers that contrasted with his white ruffled shirt, white cravat, and waistcoat of white silk brocade, her partner seemed to be the epitome of sartorial splendor.

When the waltz ended, her head was still whirling. The earl returned her to Lady Stuart's side, bowed, and sauntered off to pursue the obligations of a host. The next set was well under way before Margaret regained a semblance of composure. Sighting her daughter dancing a quadrille, she glowed with pleasure.

But the next instant found Margaret staring at her daughter's tall, bewhiskered partner. The man resembled Charles Lowndes. It was not him, of course. Indeed, the Fleet Street printer would be the last person the earl would invite. Nonetheless, the resemblance gave rise to an unwelcome revelation. Henrietta and the printer had bamboozled everyone at Countess Lieven's. When introduced to each other, they'd pretended they hadn't previously met, when in point of fact, they had. How else could he have arranged to publish her daughter's book? Furthermore, they'd taken Margaret in once again a few days later when he'd called to invite Henrietta for a drive in the park.

Her distress burgeoned as the magnitude of her daughter's duplicity — a child she'd heretofore regarded as a guileless innocent — took on a new, disturbing dimension. Her agitation grew as she divined that Lord Pardo, the man Henrietta had used so outrageously, was this very night engaged in giving a ball, solely to acquaint his relatives and friends with the shameless minx.

Margaret recoiled in horror as it dawned on her that Henrietta had patterned her villain after the earl, thus setting in train a vicious round of gossip and rumor. The thoughtless chit deserved to be spanked. Obviously she hadn't bothered to consider the possibility of serious repercussions. Didn't she realize if the earl ever found out she was the culprit, very likely he'd withdraw his support of the betrothal?

No question Henrietta was clever. What she lacked was common sense. Imagine whistling down the wind both a love match and the chance to form an excellent connection. It didn't bear thinking of, Margaret decided crossly.

"Gracious! Wouldn't you think she'd have better sense?"

Shaken, Margaret trained her gaze upon Lady Stuart. "I beg your pardon, ma'am. I confess I was not attending."

"Your sister-in-law, my dear. Such scandalous conduct. Bad enough when some of the pretty young widgeons so foolishly risk their reputations and health by wearing diaphanous fabrics and dampening their petticoats, but for a widow well past her prime to take up the practice is positively disgusting."

Margaret's brown eyes sought out the Countess of Chilsea. Spying her engaged in a country dance, she tried to judge her ladyship's attire impartially. Though the countess's salmon pink silk was cut quite low — exposing more bosom than most matrons did customarily — it didn't signify. Lady Chilsea might be sailing close to the wind, but her décolletage, while daring, stayed within social bounds. It was the material of the countess's dress that Lady Stuart was all on end about. The silky fabric was wafer thin, besides which its pale salmon hue was unhappily close in shade to a flesh color, creating an overall effect that was, to say the least, startling.

"Dear me. Here comes the brazen hussy," her ladyship complained. "I declare I'm ready to sink."

When the countess, borne on the arm of a nondescript gentleman, joined them, Margaret had further opportunity to examine Lady Chilsea's gown. The degree of transparency proved deceptive close at hand. However, even a glimpse of the countess's voluptuous figure was unfortunate, for it revealed telltale bulges that far from raising male passion seemed more apt to incur their distaste.

Margaret was momentarily overcome with a belated surge of gratitude. How lucky that her sister-in-law had refused to lift a finger on Henrietta's behalf. She now realized that Lady Chilsea's sponsorship might have been most embarrassing.

A footman bore down on Lady Stuart, drawing her off to deal with a domestic crisis, thereby leaving Margaret at the mercy of the countess, who, observing her escort deep in conversation with a cohort, pinched her sister-in-law's arm. Startled, Margaret focused her gaze upon Lady Chilsea, who awarded her a wintry smile.

"I collect you are in transports because of Lucian's marked attentions of late. But allow me to give you a sisterly hint. He's much too proud of his lineage to ever make you an honest proposal, though I don't rule out the possibility that he may offer you a slip on the shoulder."

Margaret clenched her fan. Her eyes glittered. "Why don't you mount your broomstick and fly away?"

"So the lioness has claws after all," Lady Chilsea purred maliciously, before turning to pluck her escort's sleeve. Gaining his attention, she favored him with a winning smile. "My lord, I feel in desperate need of some fresh air."

The countess strolled off, leaving Margaret shaking with barely suppressed anger, not to mention a wave of gloom that threatened to overwhelm her. What was the matter with her anyway? she chided herself. She knew better than to let her sister-in-law's acid remarks wound her. Nor would she have, had the countess refrained from broaching the subject of her feelings toward the earl. Searching the room, she caught a glimpse of him dancing with a whey-faced young miss and was much struck by his kindly attentiveness. Margaret experienced a flash of insight. Lord save her! She was in love with the Earl of Pardo!

Such a *tendre* was hopeless, of course. Utterly hopeless, even if Henrietta hadn't included a cruel caricature of him in her novel. As for herself, what a giddy peagoose she was not to have realized her feelings were engaged. But, in her defense, the thought of falling in love with Lord Pardo had simply never entered her head. In point of fact, she'd given up the idea of ever falling in love years ago — about the time she'd married John Astell. Thus, even when widowed, she'd still believed herself immune to any sort of romantic attachment. Floundering in a sea of misery, Margaret stared at the whirling figures, without really seeing more than a colorful blur.

The Earl of Pardo had completed his bow before she realized he stood before her. She swiftly lowered her gaze, afraid he might glimpse her heartache reflected in her eyes. Bad enough that the Countess of Chilsea suspected she'd ill-advisedly developed a *tendre* for Lord Pardo. If he ever learned of her regard, she'd die of embarrassment.

Lucian bore her off toward couples already poised to dance once the music resumed. Then, apparently changing his mind, led her out of the ballroom and down the hall to the book room instead. After seating her on the sofa, he retraced his steps to the door, which he firmly shut.

Dispiritedly, Margaret watched him cross to the fireplace and light split logs already prepared. Next, he opened a glass cupboard and poured brandy from a decanter into a tumbler.

He brought the brandy to her. "Here. You're pale as a ghost. Drink it all."

Margaret hazarded a cautious sip. Soon after, a trail of fire blazed upward from the pit of her stomach. However, despite momentary discomfort, the brandy revived her.

"My God, Margaret, who put that wounded look in your eyes? If that vicious sister-in-law of yours has said something to cause you pain, I'll cut out her tongue. Pay no heed to anything she says. It's all a pack of lies."

"Is it?" Margaret trained dejected eyes upon him, half-convinced he was about to offer to set her up as his mistress, but praying she was mistaken.

The earl flushed. Had Henny boasted to Margaret about their long-since-cooled affair? He wouldn't put it past her. Anything to stir up mischief. Would it soothe Margaret's ruffled feathers if he explained his affections had never been deeply engaged? Lucian decided he dare not take that chance. The present moment was too important. He captured her hands. "Margaret, I love you. Do you think you might be able to return my regard?"

"You what?" Dear God. She must be strong. For the children's sake she must never accept his *carte blanche*.

"I love you, dammit!" His voice raised to a near shout. "Oh, Margaret, I know I'm making mice feet of the business, but I can't help it. I've never offered for a female before in my life."

"Never?" she echoed. Was it possible his intentions were honorable? She felt light-headed.

"Never in forty years. So for God's sake, Margaret, will you marry me?"

"Marry you?" she echoed. She *was* going to faint.

"Oh the devil. Margaret, say you care for me. Say you'll be my wife."

Speechless, she regarded him with wary caution, trying to control her trembling lower lip.

Lucian studied her uncertainly. "Devil a bit. Do you love me or don't you?"

"Yes, I do, but . . ." Good heavens. Her treacherous tongue had betrayed her.

Before she could backtrack, Lucian had gathered her into his arms. In a moment of weakness, Margaret leaned against his firm, broad chest, feeling cosseted and quite safe. He began to caress her hair, the tips of her ear lobes, and then his eager lips sought her mouth. For a few precious minutes, she allowed herself to be swept up in his ardor, but all too soon she recalled the book her scribbler daughter had written depicting him as a villain.

Knowing what great pride the earl took in his consequence, Margaret's spirits sank.

For a few more heartbeats, she allowed herself to bask in his warmth. Then, convinced any future between them was hopeless, she struggled to be free. Very slowly, the earl loosened his embrace, although his eyes continued to regard her with tender bewilderment.

"My lord, I'm dreadfully sorry, but I cannot marry you."

"What?" he thundered, his amazement clearly visible.

Shrinking against the sofa cushions, Margaret repeated in a thready whisper, "I cannot marry you."

His black eyes bore into her until she began to fear their intensity would literally burn a hole straight through and out the back of her head.

"Let me see if I understand you. You love me, but you cannot marry me. Is that what you're saying?"

She nodded, chastened by his sarcasm, unable to defend herself. Undoubtedly, she reflected, his opinion of her had touched bottom. And no wonder. Even to her own ears, she sounded like a cotton-headed ninnyhammer.

"Why not? You're not already married, are you?"

"Indeed not," she responded with spirit. "I've only been widowed a little over a year, as well you know."

"Then why can't you marry me?"

"I . . . I cannot tell you the reason."

"What? Margaret, this is outside of enough. If you won't marry me and you love me, the very least you can do is tell me why."

"Truly, I cannot. It is a matter of scruples."

If ever there was a time when she wished her sense of ethics wasn't so nice, it was now. But she couldn't agree to be his wife without revealing the abominable trick Henrietta had played on him. Besides, her conscience would never cease to plague her if she were to purchase her own happiness at the expense of her daughter's.

Lucian, who'd been pacing furiously up and down, broke off to approach her. "Dammit, Margaret, I won't eat you. Tell me what troubles you," he shouted.

Margaret attempted to push herself further into the cushions. Instantly, the earl looked contrite and said in a calmer voice, "My poor darling. You look burnt to the socket. Sit tight. I'll fetch Aunt Min."

A few minutes later, Lady Stuart entered on her nephew's arm. With her usual tact, she didn't pry or ask Margaret any embarrassing questions. Mindful of his duties as host, the earl was obliged to leave his aunt to attend Margaret while he returned to the ballroom.

"I'm sure Lucian wished to remain at your side, my dear, but one of us must keep up appearances by mingling with our guests," her ladyship volunteered.

"I quite understand. I'm sorry to be a nuisance."

"No great matter, I assure you. Though poor Lucian is quite beside himself in regard to your distress, my dear Margaret. I'm sure you've noticed."

Dear heaven. Was she so transparent that her ladyship suspected she was in love with the earl? Or had he confided to his aunt that he meant to make Margaret an offer? Either thought put her to the blush. A fleeting, but intense, urge to wring Henrietta's pretty neck swept through Margaret.

Sometime later, mother and daughter journeyed homeward in the earl's elegant barouche. Lady Stuart had insisted on sending her own abigail along to keep a close watch over Margaret. She'd protested this scheme, of course, but as neither her ladyship nor the earl would give over, Margaret had been forced to acquiesce.

Naturally, the abigail's presence prevented her from ringing a peal over Henrietta's head, but it didn't signify. She was so blue-deviled she didn't feel up to it. Nonetheless, Margaret was sorely tempted when Henrietta leaned forward to ask, "Did you have a good time, Mama?"

13

The morning after the ball, Margaret dressed with extra care, in the hope that her new moss green muslin would draw attention away from the faint puffiness about her eyes. Upon setting foot inside the breakfast room, she discovered Enid Potts perusing the *Morning Post*.

After an exchange of the usual civilities, Enid remarked, "The paper is full of Wellington's doings today."

"Really? Do read to me, please," said Margaret, determined not to wear her heart on her sleeve.

"The fortress at San Sebastian surrendered on the ninth of September. There's talk of making Wellington a duke."

"Castlereagh's suggestion no doubt." Margaret's tone was slightly astringent. "It was he who persuaded the powers that be to make Viscount Wellington a marquess."

Enid sent her a curious glance. "You don't approve?"

She shrugged. "Whether I do or not hardly matters."

"What an odd mood you are in this morning. Surely the man deserved a raise in title after Salamanca."

Margaret gave a rueful chuckle. "You are quite right to scold, Enid. Pray disregard my ill-humored remarks. I'm a trifle out of sorts."

"You do look a bit hagged. Didn't you sleep well?"

"Not very. I think I'll have some breakfast. It may improve my temper."

Taking her usual chair, Margaret took some marmalade to spread on a piece of hot buttered toast and poured steaming coffee into a Wedgwood queen's-ware cup. "Have you seen Henrietta this morning, Enid?"

The spinster's sallow face assumed a scowl. "As a matter of fact, I saw her leave the house quite early."

"Indeed. Did she mention where she was going?"

"No. When I took it upon myself to ask, she said she had an errand to run, and bade me to tell you not to worry because she was taking Luke."

Margaret forced herself to eat a slice of toast and to drink her coffee. In truth, she didn't know whether to be glad or sorry that Henrietta was not on the premises. No secret she dreaded the impending interview, which promised to be painful.

"The oddest thing about Henrietta skipping off before breakfast was what she chose to wear." Enid's voice reflected her puzzlement.

"Oh? What did she have on?"

"A dowdy pewter blue stuff dress." Indignation flitted across the spinster's face. "And that quiz of a hat! Faded black straw with gobs of black gauze veiling. Perfectly wretched."

"Gracious. I thought she'd discarded both long since."

"And so she should have. I pray no one of consequence sees her. I shouldn't like them to hold either of us responsible her outlandish outfit."

"Quite right. However, I don't think anyone is likely to recognize her dressed like that." Margaret's temples pounded. Was she partly to blame? Had she been too lax in her dealings with her daughter? A wave of despair engulfed her as she contemplated the drab future she could look forward to in contrast to a happier life married to the earl. She gave a wistful sigh. "I daresay you are right, my dear."

The spinster's canny black eyes studied her friend's demeanor. "Last night I read that scandalous book the earl brought. Oh, Margaret, for Henrietta to make him the villain of her Gothic novel is dreadful."

"I quite agree. Especially as he's so closely related to Miles."

"Whatever made her do it?"

"I wish I knew. Though I've wracked my brain, I can't think why she served Lord Pardo such an ill turn. It may well put a period to her betrothal, though I suppose being so young and inexperienced that didn't occur to her. And when, pray tell, did she find time to write it?"

Guilt flooded the spinster's sallow face. "I did notice that she often slips up to the attic," she confessed. "I never thought to mention it before. After all, why would I suppose she'd be writing a book?"

"I must admit I'm disappointed in her. She reneged on her promise to confine her scribbling to a private journal during her come-out. Do you know, Enid, I was so angry yesterday when I found out what she'd done, I dared not call her to account."

Enid made a sympathetic clucking sound.

193

"Lord Pardo is so proud. If he ever gets wind of this, I would imagine he'll do everything he can to discourage his heir from marrying her. Pity she took a notion to kick dust in his face just when he'd climbed down from his high horse and approved the match."

"Yes, it is a shame," Margaret concurred.

"If she's scotched her chance to marry Miles Stuart, she has only herself to blame. The worst of it is she may have ruined yours as well."

"Whatever are you talking about, Enid?"

"I collect you've been preoccupied with ensuring Henrietta's future and did not notice." The spinster, attempting a smile, achieved a grimace. "I may be all about in the head, but I believe the earl entertains a marked partiality toward you, my dear. I daresay if Henrietta had behaved as she ought, he would have made you an offer."

"Obviously, you are a keener observer than I am. I never dreamed . . . not until . . . and now it's too late!"

Margaret's brave facade crumbled and she burst into tears. Embarrassed by what she considered to be an unseemly display of emotion, she impatiently tugged at her lace-trimmed sleeve, seeking the linen handkerchief tucked in the cuff.

"My dear, don't take on so. I cannot bear to see you overset," Enid pleaded.

"I did not mean to cry, truly. Yesterday, I realized Henrietta had played the earl for a fool. Then at the ball, what does he do but take me aside to pay his addresses."

Margaret cast her friend a grief-stricken look. "The most dreadful part of this sorry business is that, because of my scruples, I had to refuse him when I wanted to accept. Oh, Enid, we could have been so happy." Overcome, she sobbed afresh.

When Margaret had finally exhausted her supply of tears, she dabbed her eyes and said gruffly, "Abominable child."

"Indeed she is," the spinster agreed heatedly. "What's more, the instant she gets home, I mean to tell her that she's ruined, not only her own prospects but yours as well."

Margaret's motherly instincts surfaced. "Oh, Enid, you must not. Promise me, you'll do no such thing."

Offended, Enid sniffed. "How can you expect her to refrain from such harebrained behavior in future if you don't make her aware of the results of her mischief?"

"Please, Enid, I cannot bear for her to

know that she's wrecked my chances. You must see how very young she is. I will own I made ever so many mistakes when I was her age. Of course, I mean to tell her I know what a wicked thing she's done, and how disappointed I am that she broke her word. Believe me, Enid, that will be enough of a burden for her young shoulders to bear. If she knew all, she might be so overcome with guilt that she would go into a decline."

A brief silence fell. Given the opportunity to digest Margaret's argument, Enid's sallow face became less severe. "There's something in what you say," she admitted grudgingly. "I, too, made errors of judgment as a green girl. Henrietta's a thoughtless chit, but she's not truly wicked."

"I quite agree. The match between her and Miles may be salvaged with a bit of luck. Only think, Enid, if she knew that the earl had made me an offer I felt obliged to decline, her guilt would weigh so heavily. She might even tell Lord Stuart what she's done. No doubt, he'd cry off."

"Depend upon it, my lips are sealed. I collect you don't wish her to inform her betrothed?"

Margaret flushed guiltily. "Is that so

dreadful of me? Perhaps I am too much the managing mama, but I wish to see her comfortably settled. If she loses Miles, not only is it unlikely she will receive a better offer, she may receive none at all. If that should happen, my grand scheme will be for naught."

"Dreadful? No, indeed," Enid said stoutly. "Of course, you wish her happily wed. Indeed, anything is better than the dreary existence of a spinster obliged to be forever bowing and scraping for a pittance. Any mother with a particle of sense would condone your behavior."

After a thoughtful pause, Enid continued, "My dear, I cannot help but think that perhaps you were too hasty when you refused the earl's offer."

"Whatever do you mean? What else could I do?"

"No question, the earl's pride has been sorely pricked. Be that as it may, it seems to me if he truly cares for you, I very much doubt he'd hold you accountable for something Henrietta did."

After a moment's sober reflection, Margaret brightened perceptibly. Recalling Lucian's genuine concern the previous evening, she decided perhaps not all was lost. Once he'd noticed how overset she was, he'd been kindness itself. Did that not show his affections were engaged? Her euphoria was soon dashed. Even if he did care for her, it was too late. She'd already refused him and doubted he'd renew his offer. With a sigh, Margaret resigned herself to waiting to see how he behaved the next time their paths crossed. She refused to give up all hope. Not as long as a remote possibility existed that she might be given a second chance to tell him how much she loved him and wanted to be his wife, provided of course he was willing — just this once — to excuse Henrietta's deplorable conduct.

"Oh, Enid, I am so glad you agreed to come live with us. You're such a help with the sewing and in a thousand other ways as well. I do beg your pardon for unburdening myself at your expense."

"Pray say no more. Never shall I forget your kindness to me when I was so desperate."

"As you wish, my dear." Margaret frowned. "By the by, when you read the novel, how did you guess Henrietta wrote it?"

The sallow face flushed an unbecoming puce. "After I finished, I recalled watching her stuff the book the earl brought behind the sofa cushions, and well, I just knew."

"I, too, guessed why the book had vanished from sight the instant I'd read *Pamela's Folly*," Margaret confessed feelingly. "Imagine my shock."

"Indeed, I am amazed you didn't succumb to an attack of the vapors."

"How could I on the eve of the ball?"

"Just so," came Enid's succinct response.

Margaret rose, determined to go on with her life in her usual fashion, although depressed by the thought that but for her scribbler daughter she might now be looking forward to being loved and cherished as the earl's countess.

"I must go upstairs and see that the twins are attending to their lessons."

It was nearly half-past eleven before Margaret heard the front door opening and closing and then quick, light footsteps on the stairs. On pins and needles, she awaited her daughter's arrival in the girl's bedchamber. Suddenly, the door burst open and Henrietta rushed inside. She slammed the door and leaned against it. The ribbons of the black straw she'd worn when she'd left the house earlier dangled from one hand.

"Gracious, child! What ails you? You rushed in here as though pursued by the devil himself."

Henrietta's face registered shock. "Mama!" she exclaimed as the ribbons she held slid from her grasp. "What are you doing in here?"

Torn between anxiety regarding her daughter's distress and indignation concerning her behavior, Margaret said tartly, "I'll ask the questions if you please, miss."

"Yes, Mama," Henrietta replied in a subdued tone of voice. She staggered across the room and collapsed on the bed.

Realizing Henrietta needed time to recover, Margaret said briskly, "I shall retire to the sitting room. Join me there the instant you regain your composure."

Sitting stiffly erect on the sofa, Margaret concentrated on keeping her hands still in her lap, though she was tempted to wring them. Perhaps she should have stayed with Henrietta? No. She'd sent the twins up with hot water to bathe her face and hands, along with a pitcher of lemonade to revive her. If she'd gone instead, she wouldn't have been able to stop herself from railing at the child prematurely.

It was hard to be patient, but at long last she heard footfalls. She glanced toward the room's threshold in time to catch Henrietta's entrance. Margaret gave a brusque nod of approval as she noted her daughter had changed into an India mull cotton of sky blue.

"You wished to see me, ma'am?"

"Yes. Close the door and take a seat if you please." Henrietta did as she was asked. Once seated she eyed her mother warily.

"First of all, I should like to know where you went this morning. I feel I must warn you I shall tolerate no lies."

"Mama, I've never lied to you in my life," Henrietta exclaimed, then apparently thinking over her statement, hastily amended, "Well, almost never."

"Indeed, I am pleased to hear you haven't lost all sense of honor. However, as you broke your word to me, I hope you will excuse me for assuming that you might take a notion to fob me off with a Banbury tale."

"Mama!" The girl's voice echoed her distress which intensified as her glance fell upon the book lying upon the end table. "Dear heaven. You know, don't you?"

"I am sorry to say that I do. Henrietta, how could you do such a horrid thing?"

The color faded from her daughter's face. "I had a good reason. At least I thought I did at the time."

Margaret spoke through gritted teeth.

"So, thanks to your scribbling, the Earl of Pardo has become the latest *on-dit* amongst the *ton?*"

"Please, Mama, I can explain."

"By all means do," Margaret invited sharply.

"At our initial meeting, he behaved so condescendingly to you, Mama, that he made my blood boil. Even so, I did not yield to temptation. However, when I learned that he had conspired to get Miles's unit transferred to the Peninsula, where his life would be endangered, just so he might break up what he considered to be a misalliance, I vowed to get even."

For a time Margaret looked dumbstruck, but she said at last, "I can understand how overset you must have been if that is what you truly believed. But whatever made you think the earl would behave in such a diabolical fashion?"

"I overheard him brag about what he'd done to the Countess of Chilsea. If I were a man, I'd have called him out. Instead I . . ."

"Instead you cast him as the villain in your novel?"

"Yes, Mama."

A lengthy silence ensued as Margaret mulled the matter over in her mind. The affair was more complicated than she'd envisioned. Still it was clear that her daughter had not behaved as she ought.

"Dearest, it never answers to seek revenge. Somehow it always comes home to roost."

"I collect you mean as the earl came to know us better, he changed his mind about the match and began to shower us with kindness. Unhappily, by then it was too late to revise my manuscript."

"Exactly so." Margaret hesitated, then plunged onward. "Now, miss, perhaps, you will explain to me, how you came to write *any* book in view of your promise to me."

"I meant to keep my word, truly I did, though I cannot think you ever understood what a sacrifice you asked of me. But that's nothing to the purpose." Henrietta sat straighter, a grim look on her young face. "The truth is when we arrived in London, I quickly realized we needed more money. Charles Lowndes in Fleet Street still owed me for an article already published, so I decided to dun him in person. I took Luke," Henrietta added, in response to her mother's look of arrested shock. "During my visit, Lowndes suggested I write a novel. I, in turn, explained that I'd promised you to only write in my journal during my come-out."

"I see. Tell me, what argument did the unscrupulous Mr. Lowndes advance that persuaded you to break your word?"

"None, ma'am. You see, I did not turn down his offer flat because, to be candid, you were having no luck procuring the right invitations into Society. I was certain we were on the verge of returning to the cottage. In that event, I believed you would raise no objection to my writing a novel, using a *nom de plume* of course. One of the reasons, I decided to try my hand at a work of fiction was the money. Do you realize for a few months' labor, I can earn enough to keep us a year in the country?"

"So you began to write your book in secret up in the attic, did you not?"

"Yes, but I did not sketch in the earl until Miles left for Spain and my anger rose to fever pitch. Now, I realize how wrong it was, but I fear I did not think so then."

"I am relieved to know you have not lost all moral sensibility. However, I beg leave to tell you I consider what you did deplorable."

"I know what I did is wrong, Mama. Can you ever forgive me for breaking my promise? The painful truth is I wished to write and made excuses to appease my conscience," Henrietta admitted, a rueful expression on her pale face.

"Of course I forgive you, dearest. I know perfectly well you never meant to raise such a breeze. What I wish to stress is that it is wise to weigh considered actions beforehand and try to determine if what we wish to do may cause others pain." Margaret soothed a stray lock of her daughter's hair back into line. "There are a few other points I feel I must bring up. I collect your pretense of meeting Mr. Lowndes for the first time at Countess Lieven's soiree was a hoax."

"Very true. I was quite stunned to see him there, but quickly realized how awkward it would be if I acknowledged him. Luckily, he had sense enough to follow my lead."

"He called on us a few days later."

Henrietta nodded. "He wished to consult me regarding a business matter."

"This morning you left the house without a word to anyone as to where you were bound. You went to see him, didn't you?"

Henrietta grew visibly agitated. "To tell you the truth, I had not the smallest wish to visit Fleet today, truly I did not. However, Lowndes insisted. If only I hadn't had the ill luck to run into him at the Russian Embassy. I've been quite uneasy ever since he learned my true name and direction."

"Whatever do you mean? Has he threatened to expose you?"

"He's careful to stop short of that. However, since my first novel did so well, he keeps pestering me to write another." Henrietta raised her outstretched palms in a helpless gesture. "There seems to be nothing I can say to persuade him that I cannot possibly oblige."

"Does he realize that you modeled your villain after Lord Pardo?"

"Yes, and that I based one of the female characters on my aunt."

"Mercy! Henrietta, do you mean to say you put the Countess of Chilsea in your book as well?" Recognition lit Margaret's face. "But of course you did. You shameless baggage. I collect who she is now." Margaret frowned. "This Fleet Street printer. Are you certain you aren't romantically interested in him?"

"Absolutely not."

"But, dearest, even though your feelings aren't engaged, how can you be sure Lowndes's aren't?"

"My conscience is clear on that head. I wager it's not affection that keep him nipping at my heels, it's the plump pockets he envisions. There's nothing he desires more than having a wife scribbling away to make him rich. Thank goodness he was all business this morning. He merely wished to sweeten his offer for a second work of fiction."

"What was your answer?"

"How can you ask after the scrape I'm already embroiled in? I told him no, made my excuses, and left the premises before he could think of a fresh argument."

A stricken look filled Henrietta's young face.

"Dearest, what is it? That's the very look you had when you rushed into your bedchamber gasping for breath."

"Mama, the most frightening thing happened just as I climbed into a hack. It gave me such a scare."

"What did? For heaven's sakes, don't keep me in suspense."

"I spied an odd little man in a bowler talking to one of Lowndes's apprentices. The lad pointed in my direction, giving me the impression they were discussing me. I begged the coachman to set off at once." Henrietta's hazel eyes mirrored acute distress. "The odd creature followed me in another hack. Fortunately, I managed to lose him by emerging from the coach's other door when we got caught up in Bond Street traffic. Mama, my pursuer wore a red vest. I think he's a Bow Street Runner."

"Merciful heavens! That's all we need," Margaret exclaimed, before lapsing into a stunned silence.

14

"A lady you say. Are you certain?"

"As to that, guvner, I ain't got no inkling as to whether she be quality or not, but I'll stake me eyeteeth, that the desprit criminal in the case is a female," Wilkins stated with dogged conviction.

An arrested expression stole into the earl's eyes, as though someone had slipped past his guard and delivered him a kidney punch. "Damnation! I cannot issue a challenge to a female."

"On that head, guv, I ain't about to argue. My prime concern is me duty as an officer of the law."

The earl fixed his brooding gaze upon the Bow Street Runner, causing Wilkins's close-set eyes to skitter about the book room in a nervous fashion. "Well, man, what am I paying you for? Describe this female."

Wilkins groped inside his mangy tweed overcoat and drew out his Occurrence Notebook. Clearing his throat noisily, he proceeded to recite in a voice brimming with wounded dignity. "Owing to the fact that said female dressed in a manner to disguise her true identity, I regret to inform his nibs, that me glimms never got a peep at the slippery wench, although I be bound to own the oddity of her clothing drew me like a terrier to a rat hole."

Though extremely vexed, Lucian could not quell a sharp jab of admiration for his adversary's ingenuity in arriving *incognito* at the printshop. To be outmaneuvered by a female, while a severe blow to his pride, had its humorous aspects. His mouth curved in a grim smile.

"I trust you will not think me vulgarly inquisitive, but dammit, Wilkins, surely you must have noticed something about this female. For instance, how tall was she? How old? What exactly comprised her disguise? I suppose it is too much to hope you may have jotted down the color of her eyes and hair?"

"Aye, m'lord, for I did not get so much as a peek at neither on account of the heavy black veil wot covered her face."

"How excessively unfortunate," the earl

said dryly. "Perhaps it will save time if you relate exactly what did occur in Fleet."

"Certainly, guv." The odd little man ran a pudgy, none-too-clean finger down a page in his notebook. "Nothing out of the way happened until this morning. There I was, guv, keeping a close watch on the printshop, when wot do I see but a heavily veiled female pay off her hack and go inside. At first, I didn't pay her much mind." Wilkins's mien was defensive, despite the fact that he wasn't under attack. "I ask you, guv, how was I to guess the flash cove I had me glimms peeled for would turn out to be a female?"

When the earl seemed disinclined to comment, the Runner resumed. "Twenty minutes later, a redheaded lad, wot's called a printer's devil, slunk out the front door and sidled up to me in the alley. Never one to let the grass grow under me feet, I struck up a conversation. Seems he'd been sent to fetch a hackney for the female I'd seen go inside. 'Twas then I had a prime piece of luck. The lad let it slip she was the author of the book wot's got your back up. Let me tell you, guv, the news came like a bolt from the blue. Why you could have knocked me over with a feather."

Lucian nodded impatiently. "Get on

with it, man. After you recovered from your surprise, what did you do?"

Wilkins threw the earl a look of reproach. His nibs seemed determined to press relentlessly on, oblivious to the stress he'd sustained while engaged in his line of duty.

"Well, guv, sensing something havey-cavey afoot, I slipped the lad a guinea and bade him fetch two hacks while he wuz about it."

"So you could follow her?"

"Aye, guvner."

This information mollified somewhat the dangerous gleam in the earl's eyes that kept prodding Wilkins to speed up his account. "To make short work of this sorry business, a few minutes after the lad went back inside, I observed the female come out of the shop, trailed by a footman. Both climbed into the hack. As soon as her cab was under way, I rushed to the second hack and scrambled up beside the coachman so's to have a clear view. I followed her, not so close as to arouse suspicion, mind you, but taking pains not to lag too far behind."

The earl rubbed his hands together. "So, you managed to trail her to her destination, did you?" Lucian's deep voice was laced with excitement as he sensed that he'd finally managed to trap the person responsible for the libelous novel.

The Runner's eyes plummeted to the room's plush carpet, but he managed to utter in a strangled voice, "Begging m'lord's pardon, I lost her in Bond Street." A hint of righteous indignation crept into his tone. "Saucy little baggage slum-guzzled me."

The earl fixed him with a frosty stare. "What's this? Do you mean to stand there and tell me, you lost her trail?"

"Didn't I just say so, guv? And me thinking I'd gulled her and just getting ready to pounce." Wilkins's tone reflected his aggrievement at the unfairness of being asked to apprehend a criminal of the female persuasion, who could not be counted on to behave as the common culprit would.

"Get out of my sight, you ignorant sapskull, before I completely lose my temper and draw your cork."

Bowing and scraping, Wilkins hastily backed out of the earl's presence, leaving a trail of muttered apologies in his wake. He was about to shut the door, when his progress was stayed by the earl's shout.

"Wait!"

The Runner peeked around the door rim. "M'lord?"

"Take one of my footman with you and hie back to Fleet. I want you to keep a sharp eye trained on that printshop during business hours. When the lady pays her next call, you are to dispatch my footman to me immediately. Do I make myself clear?"

Wilkins frowned. "Begging your pardon, guv, but I prefer to work alone."

"Do you indeed? Need I remind you I am paying you to follow my orders? The second that female sets foot in that shop, send my footman to fetch me while you stay behind to keep watch."

"You intend to show up at Fleet Street in person, m'lord?"

"Depend upon it. I mean to apprehend her. I must find out why she bears me a grudge. But we are wasting time. Off with you, man. And don't you dare come back to me with any more tales about losing your quarry in Bond Street."

"Aye, guvner." Reclaiming his bowler, Wilkins beat a hasty retreat.

Still in a temper, the earl yanked the bellpull so hard a long section broke off. Staring gloomily at the frayed cording in his hand, he exclaimed, "It's all of a piece."

His expression pensive, he retreated to an oversized leather chair, barely rousing himself from his brown study when his elegant butler entered the book room in answer to his summons. His features icily remote, Lucian demanded the brandy decanter and a glass.

The butler, drawing on the fact that he'd served the Pardo family for many years, demurred. "It's barely past noon. A glass of port and a light snack might be more appropriate."

"Damnation! Am I surrounded by chuckleheads? Fetch me brandy!" His voice, raised to fever pitch, warned he would brook no further opposition.

"Very good, my lord." The butler backed his way out of the room but soon reappeared bearing a cut-crystal decanter of brandy, a glass, plus a wedge of Cheddar and a sharp knife on a round tray.

The light repast was of course a token show of defiance, still the earl let it pass, his spirits too blue-deviled to summon the energy to rail up at his butler a second time. Lucian sat for over an hour undisturbed, sipping brandy, and absentmindedly nibbling cheese.

Two weeks passed with no further word from Wilkins. Then on a Monday, Lucian woke with a sour taste in his mouth and a pounding headache. Struck blind by bright streaks of sunlight flooding the bedchamber, he muttered grumpily, "Who the devil's opened the draperies?" And when finally able to focus his gaze upon his valet despite the glare, inquired coldly, "What's the time, Partridge?"

"A bit after ten," the valet informed him diffidently.

"In the morning? Have you gone queer in the attic? What do you mean waking me at this ungodly hour?"

"I am only following your express order, my lord." Partridge's tone was long-suffering.

"Forgive my wretched curiosity, but when did I give such a harebrained command?" the earl inquired with a touch of acerbity.

"A fortnight ago. Though I beg leave to say your lordship has missed no chance to repeatedly drum your instructions into my head every day since."

Gently massaging his throbbing temples, Lucian muttered, "Pray enlighten me, Partridge. What orders are you referring to?"

"You instructed me that in the event the Bow Street Runner you hired sent your footman home, you wished to be informed at once, regardless of the hour."

"Oh, *those* orders." With a resigned sigh, the earl swung his feet over the side of the bed and sat up. Immediately, he groaned and his hands flew to his pain-wracked brow. "My apologies, Partridge, for ripping up at you. I've a curst head this morning."

"I expect you do, my lord," the valet said sagely.

Lucian sent him a rueful grin. "I gather I was a trifle castaway when I arrived at my doorstep last night?"

"Not to mince words, you were foxed. Gave me no end of trouble getting you out of your elegant garb and into your night-shirt."

"No need to parade my sins before my eyes, Partridge. I take it my footman's returned to the fold?"

The valet nodded. "Cook's giving the lad a bite belowstairs. Shall I ask her to make up a posset to settle your stomach?"

"An excellent notion. And while you're at it, order my carriage be made ready immediately. Once you've discharged those tasks, you may help me dress. I am in a tearing hurry to get to Fleet Street."

"Very good, sir." Partridge prudently refrained from the observation on the tip of his tongue, namely, that the nip in the autumn air might well serve to clear his lordship's aching head.

A scant thirty minutes later, the earl interrogated the footman in the book room.

"A female in mourning, you say?"

"Leastaways a female wearing black and heavily veiled. Her hired hack stopped smack dab in front of the printshop. A female got out and went inside. Wilkins sent me off on the run to St. James's Square to inform your lordship."

"That's all you saw? A female shrouded in black? You didn't get so much as a glimpse at her face?"

The footman shook his head. "How could I from the alley? Especially with that veil."

Frustrated, Lord Pardo decided to cut line. Dismissing the young servant, it was his intention to lose no time in running his adversary to ground in Fleet Street. However, as he strode toward the front door, Lady Stuart called to him from the breakfast room. Quelling a surge of impatience, he reluctantly reversed his direction.

Aunt Minerva nodded to him as he entered. "How good of you to bear me company this morning, Lucian. I confess I'm feeling a trifle down pin."

"I am truly sorry to hear that, Aunt Min. What's amiss?"

"Nothing I can put my finger on. It is just that I haven't heard from Miles in weeks."

"I shouldn't let it worry you. I make no doubt a packet of his letters will all come at once."

"I daresay you are right." Lady Stuart gave a deep sigh, then noting Lucian staring longingly at the coffeepot, inquired, "Shall I ring for a fresh pot?"

"Nothing I'd like better, but unfortunately I'm in a devilish rush."

"I quite understand. Pray forget I ever mentioned feeling low."

"I hope I am not so callous." Lucian bent to give her a light buss on her wrinkled cheek. "I promise to banish your megrims this evening."

She laughed. "I sincerely trust I shall have recovered my spirits long before then."

"So do I. Are you sure you will be all right?"

"Yes. Do stop fussing and run along."

"Very well then, I'm off."

Despite the crowded streets, the barouche made good time, and soon after the Strand merged with Fleet, Lucian spotted

Charles Lowndes's printshop. His eyes narrowed as they took careful note of the hack loitering at the curb, before he emerged from his carriage and sauntered over to the alley where Wilkins waited.

The Runner's eyes gleamed with relief. "Guv, you've come at last. I was beginning to worry that you wouldn't get here before our pigeon flew the coop."

"She's still inside the printshop, I gather?"

"Right you are, guv," Wilkins was quick to assure him. "Been in there well over an hour, though what business a lady has in such a place is enough to boggle me brainbox."

"I dare swear it is always difficult to fathom the workings of a female mind; however, this is no time for idle conjecture. Keep your eyes peeled while I venture inside to see if I can finally get to the bottom of this. When I emerge, I shall tug on my neckcloth if I require assistance. If I don't signal, call on me tomorrow morning in St. James's Square. By then, I shall know whether or not I require your services any longer. If I do, I'll issue further instructions. If not, I'll settle up with you."

"M'lord, 'tis me duty to warn you against entering the shop alone," Wilkins protested. "It would ease me conscience, if you give me leave to tag along. Only consider this libeler-cove is a curst slippery customer."

"I trust I'm able to manage one lone female without outside assistance."

The earl's disdain for the notion he might be unequal to the task was unmistakable as he strode toward 76 Fleet. Lucian paused on the sidewalk in front of the establishment. A fatherly looking coachman, perched on the box of the waiting hack, lifted his top hat and called out a greeting.

Lucian detoured to the public coach standing at the curb. "Good afternoon."

"Begging your pardon, yer honor, but as it's plain you mean to enter the shop, would you be so kind as to inquire of the lassie in black gloves wot hired me if she still desires me to wait?"

"A young lady attired in black? In mourning for a close member of the family, I presume."

"As to that, your guess is as good as mine. The lass ain't one to prattle."

"Close-mouthed is she?" the earl observed blandly. "As to your commission, I shall be happy to inquire as to the young lady's wishes and send out word."

"Thankee kindly, yer honor. I don't mind owning to feeling a wee bit uneasy as to her welfare. She looks to be a mite younger than my own bonny lass."

"Rest assured I'll do my best to see she comes to no harm."

"I knew you were a right'un, guvner," the coachman said gruffly.

"Humbug," Lucian muttered, as he opened the door and stepped inside.

Instantly, his senses were assaulted from all sides. Lucian's ears rang with the discordant sound of lumbering presses. His nose wrinkled in disgust as acrid ink fumes wafted up his nostrils. His eyelids fluttered up and down like distraught butterflies as his eyes worked to bring the hazy scene into focus.

When he finally got his bearings, he spotted the tall, bewhiskered Lowndes dodging heavy machinery as he headed toward a door in the side wall. Lucian watched the publisher open it and disappear inside.

An instant later, the earl stole across the murky shop to the door Lowndes had passed through. Upon reaching his destination, he was pleased to discover it stood slightly ajar. His ears perked as he recognized the printer's raised voice.

15

"Allow me to offer my profound apologies for keeping you on tenterhooks, but I fear a broken press takes precedence over all other concerns," Lowndes explained.

"Quite," Henrietta responded tersely.

"By jove, you have scarcely touched the nuncheon tray I arranged for."

"I drank a cup of tea. To be plain, sir, your rude note demanding I call upon you today has cast me up in the boughs. Is it so wonderful I've no appetite?"

Henrietta steeled herself not to fidget under Lowndes's scrunity; however, behind her pale, composed countenance, her emotions seesawed between enraged indignation that the publisher had had the cheek to send her the strongly worded missive and her mushrooming suspicion that, by fair means or foul, he meant to coerce her into writing another work of fiction —

which she was determined never to do. Bad enough she'd broken faith with Mama once, she was firmly resolved never to do so again.

"Miss Astell, I beg you to reconsider your delicate situation. Because your first novel was a sell-out, I am willing to pay you handsomely for the next. I'll go as high as two hundred and fifty pounds. You can hardly deny your family could put the money to good use."

"That's beside the point. Writing a second goes against my scruples."

"Fustian! It's a bit late in the day to try to bamboozle me." Lowndes's smirk gave way to a frown. "I've got it! One of my competitors has promised you more money? Whatever his offer, I'll better it. Now, what could be more reasonable?"

Heartsick, Henrietta decided it would do no good to explain that when dearest Mama had found her out she'd been deeply mortified. Lowndes was too crass to care about ethics. What he wanted was a second profitable work. Obviously he intended to keep on pestering her until he got his way. Whatever could she say to change his mind? Sorely pressed, Henrietta scoured her brain, desperate to find a way out of her tangle.

"You are mistaken, sir. No other publisher has made me an offer. As to the sum you propose to pay, while I cannot deny it would make us more comfortable, I hope I'm not so greedy. To be honest, I shall not write another romantic work, not even if you agreed to pay me with the crown jewels."

Scowling, the publisher fluffed his side whiskers. "I collect, Miss Astell, that Viscount Stuart is not aware that you wrote a book that has the *ton* agog."

Henrietta stirred in the Windsor chair. The wily printer was careful to couch his threats so craftily that she was left to wonder whether she merely imagined he was bent on tightening the thumbscrews, or if he was merely amusing himself playing cat and mouse.

"It is true the viscount has no inkling," Henrietta admitted dejectedly. "Doubtless, once he finds out, he will wish to cry off."

"No need for him to know ever. Though I would liefer have you wed me rather than Stuart. I vow you could write from morning till night with never a cross word from me."

"What a hum! Why should you complain when you'd grow rich as a result?"

"Very true. What do you say?"

"I say no, sir." In a high fidget, she began to pick at the voluminous veiling attached to the black straw hat that she'd worn into the printer's office and had only removed when certain she was safe from prying eyes.

"So be it. I cannot blame you for choosing a nobleman over a commoner. However, you must understand as a businessman I cannot afford to let an author with your talent slip through my fingers."

Henrietta gasped. "Sir, you are abominable."

"Come, come, Miss Astell, it won't answer for the pot to call the kettle black."

"Whatever do you mean?"

"If you refuse my generous offer, I shall call on the Earl of Pardo and expose you. Naturally, I am most reluctant to injure your prospects, but unless you agree to write a second novel, I have no other choice."

Henrietta's head spun dizzily. Her safe, secure world seemed on the verge of toppling like a house of cards. She did not mind so much for herself. After all, she deserved to be snubbed by the *ton*, but the family she loved did not. Especially not Mama.

"Very well, sir, do your worst."

"You refuse to write a second novel?"

"Most definitely. Furthermore, I beg leave to inform you I did not accept Miles's offer because of his title or his fortune, but only because I love him. Not that I expect you to understand such sentiments, for you, sir, are heartless. So go ahead, tell the earl all." Henrietta drew herself upright and proceeded to ease her trembling fingers into black gloves.

"You cannot be serious. Your reputation will be ruined. You will have to leave London. Where will you go?"

"I, sir?" She gave a brittle laugh. "I shall go home to the family cottage."

"No! I cannot allow you to escape me," Lowndes cried as his hand clamped upon her shoulder. "By Jove, if I have to, I'll keep you under lock and key until you agree."

Truly alarmed, Henrietta tried to wiggle from the printer's grasp, but his grip was too strong. Her already pale countenance turned even more ashen. Mercy! Lowndes must have gone mad! What was she going to do? She was in a devilish coil!

"Unhand her, you blackguard!" thundered Lucian as he rushed into the office.

Reacting to the earl's angry shout, the printer shunted Henrietta aside, and braced his feet against the nobleman's charge. Unfortunately for the publisher, he knew next to nothing regarding the science of fisticuffs and could barely manage a token defense. Not that it mattered. Of late, Lord Pardo, smarting from Margaret's rejection, had taken to spending a great deal of time at Gentleman Jackson's Boxing Salon. In prime condition, he had no difficulty planting Lowndes a facer.

The printer sailed several yards in the air before his backside hit the floorboards with a satisfying thump. Facial expression bedazed, he gingerly probed his jawbone, checking to determine the extent of injury.

The earl glared down at him. "By heaven, if I ever hear of you threatening Miss Astell again, I'll horsewhip you! What's more, if you ever so much as drop the smallest hint by newsprint or word of mouth that alludes to me, my family, or Miss Astell's, I vow I'll haul you before a magistrate."

"No need to climb on your high ropes, your lordship. I was only teasing the silly chit."

"Cut line. Unless you want me to tip you a settler."

The earl treated Lowndes to an icy stare. The printer shivered.

"No need for violence. In future, I vow

to give both you and Miss Astell wide berth."

As Lowndes continued to babble apologies in a placating tone, Lucian shook his head in disgust, muttering not quite under his breath, "Miserable wretch."

However, his gaze softened as it fell upon Henrietta, cowering near the desk. Lucian snatched the motley black straw from the desktop and jammed it onto the startled girl's head before he spirited her out of the printshop and into his barouche. After a quiet word with the coachman Henrietta had engaged, Lucian gave him a generous tip and dismissed the hack. Loose ends tied up, he joined her inside the carriage, and ordered his driver to set off.

As the coach bowled along, he looked askance, catching Henrietta's profile. Her normally radiant complexion was chalky. Then, shaking his head as though to clear it, he turned his perplexed gaze out the window.

Henrietta peered timidly at the nobleman seated beside her. Her spirits sank as she noted the rigid set of his shoulders. The earl would never forgive her. He'd taken the Astells under his wing in Miles's absence, and she'd repaid his many kindnesses by making him the laughingstock of the *ton*. She was so ashamed. Miles would be so hurt, so embarrassed when he found out. Naturally he'd cry off. Who could blame him?

The silence inside the moving carriage lengthened. At last, Henrietta stirred in her seat and said in a chastened voice, "My lord, I wish to thank you for coming to my rescue. Indeed, I don't know what would have become of me if you hadn't stepped in just when I thought I was at my last prayers."

Lucian snorted. "I will own I was tempted not to lift a finger. For if I hadn't interfered, you'd have come by your just deserts!"

Henrietta cringed. Tears trickled down her cheeks. She reached inside her reticule seeking a handkerchief.

Witnessing her discomfort, the earl's anger melted. "Here, use mine." He thrust a snowy square of linen toward her.

While Henrietta mopped up her tears, the earl leaned out of the coach window to instruct the driver to set them down before a confectioner's shop located just off Bond.

"My lord, I've no time to dally. Mama will be all to pieces wondering where I am."

Lucian raised one dark brow. "I can hardly return you to Upper Wimpole in your present state. Only think how nerve shattering it will be for your mother if you arrive at your doorstep looking untidy and teary eyed."

"Very well, my lord, I withdraw my objection."

Since Lucian had too much address to broach the painful topic that lay between them until after they'd finished a delicious tea, Henrietta began to relax. Her eyes swept his face before she lowered them shyly. "It is very kind of you to bring me here. I'd no idea I could swallow a morsel of food, yet once tea arrived, I found I was quite famished."

The earl laughed. "So I noticed. I must say I'm glad to see you are not one of those insipid misses who think it's fashionable to starve themselves."

Henrietta's faint smile faded. The time was ripe to square her account with the earl. "My lord, I collect you now know I wrote *Pamela's Folly*, and what is so much more reprehensible, that I modeled my villain after you."

"So I surmised once I discovered the door leading into Mr. Lowndes's office standing ajar. I must admit I stood transfixed as the gripping melodrama unfolded before my eyes," the earl said dryly.

Seconds ticked past. Henrietta could

think of nothing to say in her defense. However, before the silence grew unbearable, Lord Pardo cleared his throat. "Do you know, Miss Astell, you are probably the last creature on earth I should have suspected of such a mad-brained scheme."

Henrietta bravely met the earl's intense gaze, then losing courage, her eyes fell.

Lucian continued to glower at the contrite girl. At last, he asked, "Is it too much to ask how I managed to earn your dislike?" He swept the air in a dismissive gesture. "No, never mind. I think I understand. My toplofty manners put your back up, I suspect. Am I right?"

"Only at first. They vastly improved once we became better acquainted."

Puzzlement continued to haunt his countenance. "Do enlighten me, Miss Astell. How did I offend you?" Henrietta waxed indignant. "No need to try to cut a wheedle with me, Lord Pardo. I overheard you brag to my aunt. How could you risk Miles's neck merely to break up a match of which you didn't approve? What I did was very wrong, but I hope you will be fair-minded enough to own that I was much provoked."

Remorse banished a look of injured disapproval from the earl's features. "You are quite right to call me to book, Miss Astell. I don't like to admit what I did, even to myself, for I am deeply ashamed. But there was no need for you to seek revenge. My own conscience has nagged me to death ever since I sent Miles off into the thick of battle."

As it was abundantly clear that the earl's admission was exceedingly painful, Henrietta could not help but be touched. "Indeed, sir, I am sure we both regret our impulsive acts that caused so much grief."

"It is generous of you to say so, but I fear I can never look Miles in the eye again once he learns of my treachery."

"Really, my lord, what a poor creature you think me. I'm not a talebearer."

Puzzled surprise dominated the earl's face. "You don't intend to enlighten him, Miss Astell?"

"To what purpose? Miles trusts you. While I don't approve of what you did, I do believe you thought you were acting in his best interest. I've no wish to stir up mischief. Indeed, I will own I find revenge leaves a bitter aftertaste."

Finding himself quite in charity with the spirited minx, the Earl of Pardo cast a warm smile across the tea table. "I am so glad for this opportunity to clear the air, Miss Astell."

"So am I. Can you ever forgive me for placing you at the mercy of all the prittle-prattles?"

"I shall be happy to if you in turn will forgive my crackbrained scheme of breaking up a match by sending Miles to the Peninsula."

"Of course, I do, my lord."

Twenty minutes after quitting the confectioner's shop, the Earl of Pardo deposited Henrietta on her doorstep.

"Thank you again for coming to my rescue."

"My pleasure, Miss Astell. Let me know if Lowndes gives you any further trouble."

"I doubt he will. Do you care to come in, my lord?"

"No, thank you. I've an appointment, but please give your mother my warmest regards." Henrietta felt quite in charity with the earl as she watched his coach trundle slowly down Wimpole. Now if she'd only hear from Miles she'd be blissfully content. The five weeks' gap between letters vexed her. She frowned. Was he getting enough to eat? Was he warm and dry or cold and wet? Engaged in battle or on the march? Henrietta let out a heartfelt sigh. She missed him so much.

16

Upon reaching his town house, the earl retreated to the book room, where he seated himself in his favorite armchair. Soon after, the butler attired in satin livery entered.

"My lord, Lady Stuart desires you to join her and Mrs. Bruton."

"Tell my aunt I must decline." He was in no mood to play the gracious host. The butler's hand was on the doorknob when Lucian said, "Kindly fetch me the brandy decanter and a glass."

"Now?" Shock etched upon the longtime servant's face. "Do as I bid, then take your Friday face elsewhere. I'm in no mood for one of your sermons."

"Very good, my lord." He hastened to place the desired decanter at the earl's elbow, then quietly departed.

The earl's brow puckered. No way did he blame Henrietta. How could he when it was his own reprehensible action that had served as a goad? No question he'd deserved to be taken down a peg. For while what she'd done was outrageous, his transgression was infinitely worse.

Lucian poured brandy into a tumbler and took a sip. One thing he'd learned from this sorry affair. People were not puppets to be manipulated at his whim. The corners of his mouth twisted in a rueful smile. It had been easy to forgive Henrietta. What was much harder to do was to forgive himself.

Awareness of the door being inched open recalled the earl to his surroundings. He was honestly amazed that anyone would dare invade his sanctuary, considering that by now it was likely the entire household staff knew of his peevish frame of mind. Focusing his gaze, he recognized his aunt, a creature he was much too fond of to give a tongue-lashing, particularly one she didn't deserve.

"Come on in, Aunt Min. I won't eat you."

As she approached, he was surprised to read acute distress in her blue eyes. "What troubles you, Auntie?"

"This just came in the afternoon post." She handed him a closely written sheet of paper.

A terrible foreboding chilled his blood. "From Miles?" Lady Stuart nodded. There was a slight tremor in her bony fingers as she dabbed the corners of her eyes with a linen handkerchief. Though Lucian felt a morbid dread of the letter's contents, compassion for his aunt's distress compelled him to peruse it without delay.

He skimmed the page, then starting from the top read it again. Girding himself to meet his aunt's anxious gaze, Lucian said soothingly, "There, there, my dear. It's bad news I admit, but by no means hopeless."

"But, Lucian, Plymouth is so far from London. And Miles has been wounded."

"True. But in the arm. Which will doubtless mend with proper care."

"Humph. I dread to think of the quality of medical attention he's been receiving. As soon as I pull myself together, I shall instruct my maid to pack my portmanteau."

"I beg you to reconsider. Sir William and I will make much better time if we don't have to worry about your comfort. Which reminds me, I must send round a note so he can get his medical bag in order and be ready when I call for him in the phaeton."

"But Lucian, Miles is my eldest son. Surely my place is at his side."

"In most instances, yes. Just now what

he needs most is a reputable physician whose care can pull him through."

"You cannot mean that you expect me to wait in London tearing my hair out wondering if Miles is alive or dead?"

"Auntie, it's imperative that the doctor and I leave at once. If you insist upon coming, I shall have to take the berlin, which will hold us up. You know you are a poor traveler. Do give over. Any delay could mean his life."

Lady Stuart sighed. "You're quite right to scold. Very well, I'll stay put. Shall I ask your valet to pack your valise while you pen a note to Sir William?"

"Yes. Mind you tell Partridge to pack only the bare necessities."

Dusk was deepening by the time Lucian got under way. He'd instructed Partridge to follow at a more leisurely pace in the berlin, since a closed coach would afford his cousin the most comfortable mode of travel on the return trip.

Lucian tugged lightly on the reins, bringing the light, swift-moving carriage to a gradual stop outside Sir William's residence. The eminent physician must have been watching the road because he emerged from the front door promptly. Well bundled in a greatcoat with a warm scarf wound round his neck, the doctor wasted no time climbing aboard, black valise in hand. A terse, blunt-speaking man, totally bereft of small talk, Sir William muttered that, as he'd had little sleep the previous night, he planned to take a nap. Good as his word, the weary physician settled back against the squabs and very soon after began to snore.

Once they had left the city traffic behind, Lucian was able to give the matched pair of bays their head. As the phaeton sped into the night, the earl grimaced. For although he meant to do everything in his power to save Miles's life, if his cousin should die, Lucian conceded that whatever he did on his behalf would not have been enough. Furthermore, should such an unhappy event occur, he knew he'd always blame himself.

The earl winced. To think he'd once thought Margaret was beneath his touch. Actually it was the other way round. He was not worthy of her. No wonder she'd turned him down. Lucian drew a deep breath. While waiting for the phaeton to be readied and his clothes packed, he'd written a brief note to Margaret begging her to allow Henrietta to keep Lady Stuart company until he returned with Miles. Surely Margaret would not refuse his request. Then again, she might. He'd always prided himself that he had a reasonable understanding of females, but of late he'd begun to doubt.

Lucian let out a ragged sigh. Had it been only this morning that the Bow Street Runner had sent word that had sent him racing to Fleet, eager to find out the identity of the mysterious female who'd had the audacity to put him in her novel? Imagine his surprise to learn his persecutor was Henrietta Astell. He gave a harsh laugh. There was no point in getting himself all worked up on that head. For Miles's sake, he must keep his wits sharp. He meant to drive straight through to Plymouth, stopping only briefly at coaching stations to obtain fresh horses and get a quick bite. Lucian set his jaw in a grim line and sent a fervent prayer heavenward that they'd reached Miles in time.

Still groggy from his fitful doze, Lucian vainly tried to settle into a more comfortable position in the bentwood rocker. An utterly impossible task, he conceded grumpily as he blinked bleary eyes.

"Are you awake, Lucian?"

"I think so. Leastaways I will be in another minute."

"Then perhaps I could trouble you for a sip of water?"

Coming to his senses, Lucian jumped to his feet and moved to bedside where he laid his palm on his cousin's forehead. "Cool as a cucumber. Fever must have broken while I dozed. How do you feel?"

"Weak as a kitten and thirsty. Very thirsty."

Happy to see Miles lucid at last after an arduous week of careful nursing, Lucian felt buoyant. "Of course you are, bantling. Here, let me prop you up so you can drink." He cradled the younger man's head carefully before raising a glass to his lips.

"Be sure to take only small sips," he cautioned.

Miles did as he bade. He drank half a glass before Lucian asked, "Enough?"

"Yes, at least for now."

The earl returned the glass to the bedside table before gently lowering Miles's head back to his pillow.

"Where am I, coz?"

"Plymouth. In a quiet boarding house off the main street."

"Oddly enough the last thing I remember is lying on a cot in a chilly warehouse at dockside."

"You've been out of your head for over

a week. Sir William desired to be called, should your temperature climb any higher. Happily your fever broke instead. I don't mind telling you, I've been worried sick."

Miles managed a tentative smile. "Was it you that kept bathing my face?"

At Lucian's nod, the viscount gave a weak chuckle. "Quite a departure for such a top-lofty earl of the realm. Since when did you decide to play nursemaid?"

"Having rushed here from London at breakneck speed, I didn't propose to let you die."

"No wonder you look as though you haven't sleep in a month. When was the last time you shaved?"

Lucian ran a hand over his stubbled chin, then gave a giddy peal of laughter. "I honestly don't remember. I did take time to bathe regularly and change my linen. Once Partridge arrived in the berlin, it wasn't so bad. We took turns nursing you. Anyway, I'm not the only one who needs a shave."

Miles ran a shaky hand across his own beard, a rueful gleam in his deep blue eyes. "You're right. However, I don't feel up to it just yet."

Lucian sobered. "Miles, I cannot find the words to express my relief that you've pulled through."

"No more than I, I assure you, coz. Right now though, I'm feeling devilishly sharp set. Any chance of getting something to eat?"

"Certainly. Right after Sir William has a look at you. I daresay a sennight of nourishing food will soon have you in plumb currant. Excuse me a minute. I'll fetch the doctor."

A week later, Lucian thrust his empty plate toward the center of the coaching inn's long plank table. Easing back in his chair, he sipped coffee dregs from a stoneware mug. Though eager to get under way so they could cover as many miles as possible before the morning's crispness gave way to the threat of a snowstorm, no trace of impatience could be read in his aristocratic features.

Surreptitiously, he took careful assessment of his cousin in an effort to determine whether they should break their journey in midafternoon or push on with the aim of reaching London shortly after dusk. Lucian quelled a sigh, resigned to waiting until noon to make a final decision. Above all, it was prudent not to overtax Miles's returning strength, and this marked their fourth day on the road.

The earl wished he'd been able to persuade

Sir William to stay on and return with them; however, the physician had pleaded a backlog of sick patients with prior claims on his time. Thus, the instant Miles was clearly on the mend, Sir William had returned to London in the phaeton, leaving the slower but more comfortable carriage behind to transport the convalescent to town in easy stages.

It was almost noon when they halted at another inn and ordered a light meal while the horses rested. Ensconced in a private parlor, Viscount Stuart raised his eyes from his plate to meet the earl's concerned stare. Smiling, he asked, "Do we have time for me to eat another trout?"

A bemused grin lightened the earl's sober mien. "Why not?" He called over a serving girl and ordered another serving.

"Certainly, yer honor. Cook'll pop one into a skillet straight away." She hurried off.

The earl's grin widened as he watched his cousin slather butter on a slice of bread. "Do save a bit of room for the trout."

"I regard this as a small appetizer to stave off my hunger until my trout appears," Miles replied, with smiling equanimity. "I'm anxious to put some weight on my bones so I won't look like a curst skeleton in Henrietta's eyes."

"Quite right. It would never do to shock your fiancée," the earl agreed.

"How was she when you saw her last?"

Lucian eyes twinkled. "Up to her ears in mischief as usual."

"Oh? Here I thought she'd be fretting herself to death because I was wounded."

The earl's demeanor sobered. "Make yourself easy on that head, Miles. I make no doubt she was very distressed by the news. However, since I felt it was of paramount importance to reach you as quickly as possible, I did not feel I could spare the time to pay her and her mother a personal call before I left town. I sent round a note instead."

"I quite understand. But it's hard to be patient. I cannot help but worry she may have fixed her attentions elsewhere."

"Do not be nonsensical. Rest assured she is attached to you all right and tight." Lucian's face took on a somber cast. The time had come. It would be unscrupulous to put off his confession any longer. "Miles, there's something of a serious nature I feel honor-bound to discuss."

"Such a glum face. I trust Henrietta hasn't fallen into a scrape."

The earl's smile was tinged with irony.

"Nothing I could not handle. She's a taking little minx. However, it is not Henrietta's conduct I wish to talk about. In point of fact, it is my own."

A serving girl plunked a platter of trout before Miles, but he was too intrigued to notice. "Really, coz, it is too bad of you to keep me on tenterhooks."

"I'm finding it difficult to make of clean breast of my deplorable conduct."

"Lucian, what are you talking about?"

"Patience, cousin. The tale will go faster if you do not interrupt."

"Very well, go on."

"To be candid, I didn't take to the Astells initially. It was only after you left to join Wellington that I grew fond of them. I must say once I came to know your betrothed better, I realized she was not a fortune-hunting social climber as I'd thought, but an intelligent, unexceptional young miss who was sincerely attached to you."

"I could have told you that."

The earl waved his cousin to silence with an imperious gesture. "Miles, I hope you will forgive me for meddling in your affairs. The truth is I pulled strings to get your unit transferred. I was convinced you two would not suit. I was mistaken. Thank goodness you will recover from your wound. Had you died, I'd have had it on my conscience the rest of my days." The earl glowered at his cousin. "Pray do not sit there with your tongue between your teeth. Say something."

"Climb down off your high ropes, Lucian," the viscount advised coolly. "*You* sent me off to battle, not the other way round."

"I beg your pardon," the earl said contritely. "It was my curst arrogant pride that steered me wrong. Can you ever forgive me?"

"Gammon! What a piece of work you're making of this. Of course, I forgive you. No great harm's been done after all."

"No harm? Miles, you almost died."

"Rubbish. As for helping Wellington lick the French, I'm proud I had a part in it. Now can we bring down the curtain on this subject?"

"By all means. Eat your trout so we can get under way."

Taking his cousin's suggestion to heart, Miles wasted no time attacking the fish before him with obvious relish. The earl lapsed into thought. Naturally, he was grateful that Miles had forgiven him so readily. Not that he was sure he'd ever forgive himself. Still it was a great load off his mind.

Soon Henrietta and Miles would be reunited. Lucian wished them happy, of course. He tried to suppress a twinge of envy but had no luck. If only Margaret would reconsider his suit. Why had she refused him in the first place if she loved him as she claimed? Margaret had said it was a matter of scruples. Scruples?

Devil a bit! His brow cleared. But of course. What a slowtop he was not to have realized it sooner. A brash grin spread gradually across his face. As if he'd hold her to blame for her daughter's action. A wave of affection swept through him. Dearest Margaret. How he adored her.

"I have scraped my plate clean, Lucian. Shall we go?" Pulling himself firmly back to the present, the earl studied his cousin conscientiously. "We need not press on if you are too tired."

"Fustian!" the viscount scoffed. "I'm fit as a fiddle. Come, I'm eager to complete the last leg of our journey."

"So am I," Lucian confessed with a laugh. The understatement of the century, he reflected as he climbed back into the berlin. Truth be told, he was in a fever of impatience to get to London so he could call on Margaret.

17

Margaret's hand shook as she broke the seal on the note the footman had just delivered from St. James's Square. Written in a bold scrawl she recognized immediately, it informed her that the earl's barouche waited at the curb to transport Henrietta to his town house to see Miles. In addition, he advised Margaret of his intention to call on her at eleven o'clock sharp. However it was the cryptic postscript that tantalized: "P.S. Have I failed to mention the family motto is: Hope springs eternal?"

Whatever did he mean? Bewildered, Margaret reached into a concealed pocket of her dress and pulled out the missive he'd sent three weeks ago, shortly before embarking for Plymouth. He'd made reference to hope in that note, too. Although she already knew the contents by heart, she carefully unfolded the wafer-thin, much-creased page and quickly scanned it.

My dear Margaret,

Miles has suffered a wounded arm. I leave within the hour for Plymouth. Aunt Min is in a rare taking. I beg you to allow Henrietta to bear her company at St. James's Square in my absence. In regard to our recent tête-à-tête, I live in hope you will undergo a charge of heart.

Yours, Lucian

Her pulse quickened. Dared she hope? Perhaps the future was not as black as she'd assumed. Ever since her daughter had made a clean breast of her confrontation with the earl at the Fleet Street printshop, Margaret's emotions had been in turmoil. Certainly Henrietta appeared convinced that the nobleman was prepared to let bygones be bygones. Still Margaret didn't know what to think. While grateful to him for his sensitive handling of her daughter's outrageous conduct, she was afraid to read too much into either note.

She gave a wry smile. If Lord Pardo's motto was "Hope springs eternal," hers appeared to be "Better safe than sorry." Timid soul that she was, she felt it would be a mistake to grow overly optimistic. Just imagine how devastated she'd be if she were mistaken and the earl did not return her regard. Her eldest daughter's quick, light step came as a welcome distraction. She hastily folded both notes and stashed them back into her pocket.

"Did Enid tell you the earl's carriage is out front?" she asked the instant she sighted Henrietta.

"Yes, she did. Mama, you've surpassed yourself. My new pelisse is all the crack."

"Dearest, I don't mean to nag, but I wish you would remember to express yourself in more ladylike terms."

"I beg your pardon. It's just that I'm so taken with my newest ensemble."

With critical eyes, Margaret examined the girl's high-waisted, ankle-length coat. Made of crushed velvet in a rich burgundy, it buttoned to her throat and had long fitted sleeves that puffed at the shoulders.

"The white fur trim is what sets it off," Henrietta proclaimed with a pardonable touch of pride. "I daresay Miles will hardly recognize me in such a dashing turnout."

Margaret couldn't quite squelch an unbecoming surge of smugness. She'd purchased the ermine pelts dagger cheap at one of the dockside warehouses and, by

251

happy chance, had decided at the last minute not to snip off the black tail tips. The result was both stylish and charming.

"Indeed, dearest, if I do say so myself, you do appear to be in the first kick of fashion."

"Good. My confidence could use a boost today." Henrietta's sunny smile was replaced by a look of distress. "Mama, I am scared. Suppose Miles no longer cares for me?"

"Peagoose. Even if his affections were not already fixed, you look so delectable, he's bound to fall in love with you all over again."

"I hope you may be right. I must be going," Henrietta said, shoving her hands into a white fur muff that matched her hat and the trim on the collar and cuffs of her pelisse. "The earl will be cross if I keep his horses standing."

A slight frown disturbed Margaret's creamy brow. "But it's so early. Scarcely the fashionable hour to call."

"Little I care for that. If I have to wait much longer to see for myself that Miles is on the mend, I am persuaded I shall go into a decline. Besides, the barouche waits at the curb. I'm expected."

Margaret glanced into her daughter's pleading eyes and gave in. "It seems I've been outmaneuvered. Run along, but take care you don't wear out your welcome."

"No fear of that. I doubt Miles is up to a lengthy visit. Now I really must go." Dropping a light kiss on her mother's cheek, Henrietta sailed from the room.

Margaret was amused by her daughter's unseemly haste. Obviously, the poor child had been afraid she'd raise further objections. She gave a rueful chuckle. Little does she suspect, I've my own worries to contend with. For example, what shall I wear when the earl comes calling? Something demure, yet ravishing, would do nicely. Mounting the stairs, Margaret hoped against hope she'd discover such an unlikely combination hanging in her closet.

Henrietta sat primly erect on an upholstered settee in the vast anteroom of the earl's town house. To her sorrow, the snobbish butler had insisted upon bearing off her smart new pelisse along with her white fur hat and oversized muff.

Impossible to cut a dash wearing an unexceptional walking dress of twilled gabardine, Henrietta decided. Oh well, at least she was warm enough. The thought cheered her up a little, for it was such a bitterly cold November day, it wouldn't surprise her if it snowed. She ran a finger across the fine wool material. Actually, her midnight blue gown with Brussels lace collar was very becoming. She just had a bad case of the fidgets was all.

Laboring mightily to call her jumpy nerves to order, she reasoned that to concentrate her thoughts on the shaky state of her relationship with Miles would send her straight up into the boughs. Instead, she trained her mind upon Lady Stuart and immediately felt calmer. Thank goodness she'd had the sense to make a full confession to Miles's mother during her stay at St. James's Square. Now all she had to do was muster the courage to tell Miles. However, she didn't wish to worry about what she was going to say beforehand. It would only make her nervous.

She sighed. Undoubtedly by this time, the earl had related the whole of her ignominious conduct to Miles. More likely than not, once apprised of what she'd done, he'd wish to cry off. The shuffle of approaching feet caused her to glance toward the archway just as the earl's butler, splendidly attired in blue livery trimmed with gold braid, crossed the threshold.

"Please follow me, Miss Astell. The earl wishes to speak to you in the book room before you go up to see Lord Stuart." He unbent so far as to issue a slight smile.

The butler tapped lightly on the book room door. A gruff voice bade them enter.

"Miss Astell, my lord," he announced before he withdrew.

The Earl of Pardo folded the newspaper he'd been reading and set it aside. Rising, he greeted her with a broad smile that put paid to the remote cast of his features in repose.

"Delighted to see you, Miss Astell."

"Thank you. How is Miles?"

"Definitely on the mend. Although the trip tired him, I expect he'll soon recover his stamina."

"What about his arm?"

"It's now healing properly. Fortunately, the infection that caused Miles's raging fever has long since subsided. The doctor cautions his arm will be stiff for a time. Eventually, Miles should regain full use, or nearly so, provided he is careful not to overtax himself."

"I'm so glad he's better." Henrietta frowned. "How did he react when you told him what I did?"

The earl awarded her a rueful look. "I did not tell him. Like you, it's not my style to carry tales."

Henrietta sighed. "I daresay I must then. If only I could be certain he won't cry off. I love him, you see."

"I doubt he'd take such a drastic step."

"Kind of you to try and raise my spirits, my lord. Still there's no telling how he'll react in advance. I shall just have to take my chances. When may I see him?"

"I shall take you to him in a minute. A word of caution first. Do not stay above an hour. He tires easily." Lucian issued one of his charming smiles. "I can hardly expect *him* to be the one to send you away, can I?"

"Indeed, I should hope not, my lord." The hazel eyes danced. "Rest assured the instant I notice his energy flag, I shall invent a plausible excuse and come away."

The earl cast her a look of approval. "My cousin perked up whenever the post brought one of your letters to him in Plymouth. I vow you had as much to do with his recovery as Sir William."

"Of all the brummish tales. I collect you continue to regard me as a green girl likely to swallow such nonsense."

"I see I must take into account the fact that you have lived in London long enough to acquire a little town bronze." He delivered another charming smile. "Come, I'll take you to Miles before the cawker grows too impatient."

Minutes later, at the threshold, Lucian gave Henrietta a gentle nudge, then strode off. Engrossed in a book, Miles remained blithely unaware he had company.

Shaken by his altered appearance, Henrietta was grateful to have time to recover from her shock before he espied her. He'd lost a lot of weight, at least a stone. His aristocratic features seemed elongated, no doubt because his illness had cruelly stripped flesh from his face, giving it an alarming gauntness. A searing wall of pain encircled Henrietta's heart, setting in motion a plethora of fresh worries, in spite of the earl's assurances that Miles was on the mend and would soon regain his full strength and vigor.

Belatedly sensing her presence, Miles's intense blue eyes lit up. "Henrietta!"

"Miles," she cried, quickly spanning the distance between them. Nevertheless, upon reaching his bedside, she hesitated. Though her first impulse was to throw herself into his arms, she worried that even a gentle embrace might hurt his bandaged right arm.

Closing the book he'd been reading and placing it on a table next to his bed, Miles reached out his left hand to capture hers. He raised it to his lips, refusing to part with it after the warm salutation. "Sweetling, what a delectable treat you are for these impatient eyes."

"Fustian," she, scoffed, barely able to manage a tremulous smile. "It is so good to have you home."

Miles wasted no time using his left arm to draw her close so he might kiss her. Though soon rendered breathless by this loverlike strategy, Henrietta was reluctant to put up any resistance, fearing an abrupt withdrawal might cause pain to his injured arm. However, a combination of guilt pangs engendered by the conviction that a proper young miss did not carry on so lengthily and with such abandon while alone in a man's bedchamber — engaged or not — plus the fact that her random gaze chanced to alight on the book lying on the night table, caused her to draw gently, but firmly, out of reach.

Miles's glance fell upon same book, before he fixed Henrietta with a piercing stare. "Guilty conscience, love?"

She gave an involuntary jump. "Wh— whatever do you mean?"

"You know perfectly well that I refer to *Pamela's Folly*, the novel you wrote." He spoke quietly, but the rigid set of his jaw signaled his displeasure.

Every nerve in her body tautened. Henrietta was convinced that what transpired in the next few minutes would seal her fate. Fighting a foreboding sense of doom, she said with a touch of resentment, "The earl intimated he didn't tell you."

"He didn't, Mama did."

Henrietta released a shaky sigh. "How I wish she had not. I intended to tell you myself, once you were better." Pensive hazel eyes scanned his drawn face. Failing to glean any hint of what he was thinking, she doggedly stumbled on. "Your cousin has forgiven me for treating him so shabbily. The question is, can you?" She took a deep fortifying breath and hastened on before she lost her courage. "Naturally, if you wish to cry off, I shall understand."

"Cry off?" Miles looked shocked. "Don't talk rot. I love you. Mind you, putting my cousin in your novel was birdwitted, but I venture to say Lucian's high-in-the-instep pride put your back up."

"It did. However, I should never have made him my villain for such a paltry reason. It was only when I learned he'd dared place your life in danger that I decided to take revenge."

The corners of Miles's mouth twitched, though he did his best to hide his amusement. "No doubt his meddling in our affairs served as an irresistible goad."

"Exactly so."

The viscount gave an appreciative chuckle. "I must admit Lucian deserved a set-down."

"Oh no, you are too harsh, Miles. It never entered my head that the *ton* would recognize him."

"I should hope not. However, what's past is past. Useless to dwell on it." Miles gave her hand a gentle squeeze. "I'm much more interested in your future conduct. I want you to know I intend to be a reasonable husband. Should you wish to continue writing once we marry, I've no objection."

She eyed him thoughtfully. "You don't seem very surprised to learn I'm a secret scribbler. How long have you known, Miles?"

"Always." His eyes danced. "Ned blabbed your history during the coach ride from Harrow." He shot her a knowing grin. "My love, the first time I saw you, I own I was quite taken by the ink smudge on your adorable nose."

Henrietta flushed. "If you knew at the onset, how come you never so much as dropped me a hint?"

"I did on at least one occasion. The reason I didn't press the point was because the subject seemed to discomfit both you and your mother."

She nodded gravely. "From the first, I wanted to tell you, but I was afraid you'd disapprove. Mama warned me no eligible suitor would offer for a young lady who wrote."

"While I hold your mother in the highest esteem, in this instance she's quite wrong," he said gently. "However, since I don't fancy being constantly obliged to fight duels, I trust you will refrain from putting any more thinly disguised members of the *ton* into your books."

"I shouldn't dream of it." Tears welled in her eyes. Miles truly did not mind she was a scribbler. Never had she been so happy, not even the night he'd proposed. Blinking his dear face back into focus, she caught him in the act of trying to stifle a yawn. The poor man was tired. "High time I took my leave so you can rest."

"Please don't go just yet. You've hardly been here a half hour," he protested.

She smiled at him fondly. "I'll stay until

you fall asleep. Does that suit you?"

"I trust I don't intrude," the earl said from the threshold.

"Of course not, Lucian. Do join us," Miles invited.

"My lord, I told Miles about the mischief I caused, and he's forgiven me."

The earl laughed. "I expected no less from my cousin."

Henrietta rose. "I'd best withdraw so Miles can rest."

"No, stay a minute," Lord Pardo urged. "I've something to say to you both."

"What's on your mind, coz?" the viscount inquired.

"First off, allow me to wish you joy. I sincerely trust you will be able to keep this shameless baggage in line. By God, Miles, you're a brave man."

"And a lucky one, too, I vow," the viscount responded.

"Yes, well that remains to be seen," Lucian teased.

"That is too bad of you, my lord," Henrietta complained in mock anger.

The earl's dark eyes brimmed with mischief. "As you will soon be part of my family, I suppose I must cry pardon. Aunt Min sent me to invite you to join her for nuncheon while Miles takes a short nap.

That way, you lovebirds can get in a second visit before you part for the day. As for myself, my phaeton awaits. However, before I go, I feel I should inform you, Miles, not to count on inheriting my title and my fortune. You see, I intend to pay my addresses to Margaret Astell, and should she consent to be my wife, I mean to do my damnedest to beget my own heir."

"My lord," Henrietta protested faintly, her cheeks rosy.

"Your plain speaking has put my betrothed to the blush, Lucian," the viscount pointed out.

"I apologize." Lord Pardo made her a slight bow. Henrietta's good-natured giggle caused the earl's lips to curve at the corners, though his face sobered when he shifted his gaze back to Miles. "Well, coz, now's the time to voice any reservations you may harbor."

The viscount awarded his cousin a sweet smile. "Rest easy, Lucian. Since I already have both, I've no great hankering for either your title or your blunt. As long as I have this scribbling brat beside me, I'm content."

"After I speak to Margaret, I may stop off at the *Morning Post.* If so, shall I tell them to print a formal announcement of your betrothal?"

"Why not? It'll save me the trouble."

"I'm off then."

Feeling more lighthearted than he had in years, the earl climbed up into his high-perch phaeton and drove at breakneck speed all the way to Wimpole. When Jonas opened the front door, the earl impatiently brushed past the slow-moving butler, thus surprising Margaret in her elegant sitting room, where she sat retrimming her second-best bonnet.

Lucian said nothing. He just grinned. Finally, maddened by his silence, Margaret asked, "You wished to speak to me, my lord?"

"Most emphatically. Dammit, Margaret, you knew when I proposed to you that Henrietta had put me in her book, didn't you?"

"Of course I knew. It's why I felt obliged to refuse you."

"Why didn't you tell me what she'd done?"

"How could I? Not only did I fear you'd withdraw your approval of her betrothal to Miles, I was also afraid it would give you a disgust of me, for after all there's no denying I am her mother."

"My foolish darling, you must learn to

trust me," he chided gently. "How could you think I'd let that vengeful baggage's prank divide us?"

Hope radiated from Margaret's face. "Henrietta did say you'd forgiven her the day you came to her rescue in Fleet," she admitted.

"Naturally, I forgave her. To be sure it was a wicked trick she pulled."

"I quite agree. It was very generous of you to overlook it, my lord."

Lucian chuckled. "To tell the truth, at first I was breathing fire. But once I'd had a chance to mull the entire matter over, I realized I only got the comeuppance I deserved."

"What of your cousin, my lord? I've been on pins and needles all morning wondering if he cried off once Henrietta worked up the courage to tell him?"

"No such thing, my sweet. Crazy young fool is determined to wed her anyway. I gave him my blessings."

Overwhelmed with tender regard for his beloved, Lucian used his index finger to coax her chin upward. When their gazes met, he felt as if he were drowning into Margaret's limpid brown eyes, then sternly recollecting the express purpose of his call, he stated sternly, "And now, madam, I believe you and I have some unfinished business to settle."

"We do?"

"Devil a bit. Bad enough you turn me down once for the sake of your skip-brained daughter, but now that that's behind us, I hope you don't mean to serve me so cruelly again."

Happiness shone from Margaret's eyes. "No, indeed. I should never have dreamed of refusing you, but for Henrietta's prank."

"You reassure me, my love." The earl watched her expression carefully. "You will marry me then?"

Heart mirrored in her gaze, Margaret swallowed nervously, then managed to say, "Yes, my lord."

"My dearest love, that's more like it."

With a rakish grin, the earl gathered Margaret into his arms and kissed her soundly.

The employees of Thorndike Press hope you have enjoyed this Large Print book. All our Thorndike and Wheeler Large Print titles are designed for easy reading, and all our books are made to last. Other Thorndike Press Large Print books are available at your library, through selected bookstores, or directly from us.

For information about titles, please call:

(800) 223-1244

or visit our Web site at:

www.gale.com/thorndike
www.gale.com/wheeler

To share your comments, please write:

Publisher
Thorndike Press
295 Kennedy Memorial Drive
Waterville, ME   04901